UNINVITED GUEST

BRIAN LANCASTER

Published by

DREAMSPINNER PRESS

5032 Capital Circle SW, Suite 2, PMB# 279, Tallahassee, FL 32305-7886 USA
www.dreamspinnerpress.com

Uninvited Guest
© 2015 Brian Lancaster.

Cover Art
© 2015 L.C. Chase.
http://www.lcchase.com
Cover content is for illustrative purposes only and any person depicted on the cover is a model.

ISBN: 978-1-63476-701-9
Digital ISBN: 978-1-63476-702-6
Library of Congress Control Number: 2015911628
First Edition November 2015

Printed in the United States of America
∞
This paper meets the requirements of
ANSI/NISO Z39.48-1992 (Permanence of Paper).

CHAPTER 1
CRASH

AN HOUR'S drive north out of Newquay and the northbound traffic slowed to a procession. Anton thumped the Audi's dashboard in frustration and dislodged the plastic Manami-Neko figurine—the red, white, and gold waving cat supposed to bring good luck—stuck there with Blu-Tack. Not that he had ever really liked the gift from his niece. Whenever the frowning feline caught his eye it felt as though the single moving arm was cautioning him to slow down. His trusted car satnav—satellite navigation—had predicted congestion on the A30 but had not recommended an alternative route. Temporarily distracted by the hunk in a silver Porsche who had been trailing him since the Bodmin turnoff and had slowed to check him out while overtaking, he now found himself two cars behind, blinking into the brake lights of a tall windowless van, a sheer white wall on wheels.

Leaving as late as he did meant having barely enough time to get home, shower, and change before meeting Paul and Julie. Racing along the dual lane carriageway had kept him focused, his concentration fixed on nudging the speed limit. Slowing to a crawl now allowed unwelcome thoughts to catch up. And right now he felt like a traitor. Gemma's eyes had said as much when he made his excuse about beating the traffic and left her to deal with the last of their relatives. Chances are, though, if he had agreed to stay another couple of nights they would end up getting sloshed together, and he might be tempted to tell his sister a few home truths about her perfect second marriage.

"Bugger," he muttered to himself as the line finally came to a halt. Four fifteen. Even without further holdups and pushing the speed limit, the journey would take at least another four hours. Meeting up at nine would be a stretch.

With an audible sigh, he let his shoulders sag and thought about phoning Gemma, but instantly dismissed the idea. Instead he resorted to refastening the cat before taking out his frustration on the automatic search button on the car radio. Each stop between the silences provided only bursts of nerve jangling static. On the off chance, he prodded the button beside the CD slot still jammed with a calming jazz compilation, but as expected, nothing happened. After seizing up a couple of months back, he still hadn't bothered to get the function fixed. Eventually he thumped the device off and settled for silence.

Ripping a scented tissue from the box on the dash, he scrubbed at a random grease mark on the steering wheel while raking through his sister's parting words. No doubt she would have labeled the snarl-up karmic retribution for going against her wishes. All she had asked was for him to stay on an extra night or two after their grandmother's funeral to spend more time with her and Ewan, the new husband, while the ex had the kids for the week. Their conversation at the garden gate had been the most they had spoken all weekend.

"Can't you stay until Wednesday? Pretty please," she had said to his back as she lounged against the garden gatepost, watching him toss his luggage into the boot of the car and slam down the lid.

"I need to get back. If you'd told me sooner, I might have been able to move things around."

"And if you hadn't noticed, I've been busy. Come on, Ant. I'm cooking Gran's mutton and Guinness pie tonight. One of your favorites."

Over jeans and a plain red woolen tee, she wore her professional chef's apron of navy with thin white vertical stripes, blemished at the waist by floury smudges. Their grandma had tried to teach them practical skills over and above their academic studies; Gemma, the art of cooking, and Anton, gardening. Gemma had surpassed Anton, and the apron had been a gift on Gemma's thirteenth birthday, something his sister dragged out and modeled when cooking for guests. Straight auburn hair identical in color to his, pulled back today by a glossy bronze hair band, stopped just short of her shoulders. In fact, even the aquiline nose, full lips, and slate gray eyes resembled his so much that in childhood they had often been mistaken for twins. Remarriage agreed with her. She had shed pounds since and, on the surface at least, appeared happier and more relaxed than ever. All afternoon, while Anton chauffeured the old folks around, she had busied herself cleaning house and preparing food.

"Cab's picking Millie up first thing in the morning. The rest are getting the train," she continued, brushing random speckles from her chest. "So we could have some us time and catch up properly. I haven't even had a chance to tell you yet. I caught Aunt Ida in the kitchen on Saturday evening, drunk as a lord, doggy-bagging sausage rolls and mini beef and horseradish buns into her handbag. Good job the wine cabinet was locked."

"Honestly, Gem. I can't even begin to find that funny," he replied, spinning around to face her, irritated by the pixie grin on her face. "At a funeral gathering. They're all as bad as each other. I still don't understand why you invited them to stay. The only time I ever heard Grandma curse was when she talked about outliving her bottom-dwelling family. She'd have been content with her small church group."

"And I invited them too, but I decided she deserved a full house for a send-off," she said, folding her arms tight the way she always did when she became defensive. "Anyway, I could hardly *not* have invited Great Aunt Millie. After that it was only a matter of time before word got out. And before you say anything, I was not about to snub her sole surviving sister."

"Even though it meant going against Gran's wishes," he muttered, more as an aside. A silence followed his remark about their late grandmother's explicit request, the only one Gemma had not honored and one the lawyer in him had argued to uphold.

"She's not here anymore, Ant. She doesn't care. This was for us, a way to celebrate who she was and what she meant to us all. Now the funeral's done and the will's settled, end of chapter. Apart from Christmas cards, we're unlikely to hear from any of them again."

"Thank heavens for small mercies."

"Anyway, back to the point. Stay on a bit longer and we can open a bottle or two of champers and celebrate her life properly. This weekend's been worse than managing the kids. Finding places to put everyone up, ferrying them back and forth, keeping them fed and sorting out the catering for the gathering—"

"Without one word of thanks."

"At one point I thought I was a Saga holidays rep for senior citizens, waving my umbrella in the air, pointing the way to the Chapel of Rest."

"You should have checked a few in."

"Ooh. Bad, bad brother," she said, chuckling and shaking her head. "You see, we need time together to cheer each other up. Stick around. There's a trendy new gay bar in town. Bar One-Nine-One. There's no way on earth I could drag Ewan along on his own, but if you come we could all have a hoot together."

Anton patted his inside pocket to check for his wallet before walking to the front gate and bending to collect his small backpack.

"Do you know what gay men think about heterosexual couples going to gay bars? That they're trying for a threesome, acting out some bisexual fantasy or another."

"Rubbish. They go for the cocktails and the music. More to the point, I can screen potentials for you. Finally get you a decent husband."

"I don't need—" he began defensively, standing and sighing and hating himself for instantly reddening at the mention of the subject. "People can exist perfectly fine on their own without the pressure and worry of having another person in their lives to care for. Look at Gran. She lived a full and happy life for years after Granddad passed away."

"She told you she was happy?"

"Not in so many words."

"Well, she told me she missed him every day. As a species, we're not designed to live our lives in isolation. I heard that on a kid's science cable channel, so it must be true."

4

He stopped before her and rolled his eyes.

"You just want it to be true. Anyway, it's different for you."

"Oh, this should be good," she said, folding her arms again, her voice lowering. "Come on, then. How is it different for me?"

"You already have a mountain of responsibilities. One more is no big deal."

"Listen to yourself, Ant. Talk about Mr. Cynical. You make it sound as though it's a one-way street. What about the responsibilities Ewan's taking on? They far outweigh my end of the deal."

"Yes, but he gets you."

"My point exactly! God, you can be really obtuse for one of your people."

In the process of pointing the car remote at the vehicle, he stopped to aim a mock sweet smile at her. Gemma, however, wasn't letting up.

"Come on, Ant. You know we have other stuff to sort out. Like what we're going to do with her house and belongings. And it's not as though you have a job to run back to."

"I'm not running back. God, you're infuriating," Anton replied, throwing his rucksack onto the backseat and slamming the door. With a huff, he thumped his back against the car door and fiddled with his car keys. "I told you. The agents want me on standby. Penny said they had a few tentative inquiries from smaller firms."

"Is this the same Penny who told you nobody recruits lawyers before Christmas?"

"Solicitors, Gemma. In England I am a solicitor. They have lawyers in the States," he said, peering up and seeing her on the pavement, leaning back against the garden gatepost, arms tightly folded. She wasn't going to give in without a fight. "Didn't you used to be a fan of *Law and Order*?"

"This is about Ewan, isn't it?"

"Don't be daft," he said, his smile slipping. On impulse he pushed away from the Audi and stood before her, looking at her collar, her shoulder, her fringe—anywhere but her eyes. "Look, he and I are never going to be best buddies. I realize he provides for you and the kids, and he seems to make you happy. I do get that, Gem. Honestly I do. We're just different people, on different wavelengths. He's into warm beer, TV snooker, and you. I'm more of a pinot grigio, *Downton Abbey*, and Tom Hardy kind of guy."

"Very droll," she said, smirking weakly and plucking a random speck from his black Scissor Sisters T-shirt. "I'm only trying to bring us closer as a family. Especially now Gran's gone. You got on with Trevor well enough."

"Your ex-husband, for all his faults, was not a homophobe."

"Neither is Ewan. Yes, he's a little rough around the edges, but he's harmless."

"Surely you're not deaf to his less than subtle remarks about 'you gays.' In front of the kids too. As though I'm part of some deviant cult."

"He thinks he's being funny. Give him time. Let him get to know you. He likes you."

"Is that what he told you?"

"Yes," she said, pulling his chin up to bring their eyes level and nodding. "He did."

Her affirmation, intended to make him feel better, had the opposite effect. But she had called him out right. Anton did find Ewan uncultured and irritating, but his bigoted jibes fell on deaf ears. What she had no idea about were the three occasions Anton had stayed over in their spare bedroom, when Ewan had appeared late at night or in the early hours of the morning to engage in one trivial conversation or another. Stark-bollock naked each time, he had lounged in the open doorway, and on this morning's occurrence he had sported a somewhat impressive semi-erection. Granted, the man had a good body, but Anton had no idea what to make of his action. Neither did he have the courage or desire to confront him and find out, preferring instead to avoid any repeat of the situation.

"I'll try to get back the week before Christmas. When the kids are home."

"Ewan's in our lives now, Ant," she said, while Anton stepped away and walked around to the driver's door. "Make a bit more of an effort, will you? For me."

Up until then Anton had managed to keep his mood neutral, but that particular plea was ill chosen.

"Like you did with Christian?" he asked pointedly, the words out before his brain engaged, and ones he immediately regretted. His ex-boyfriend had been a constant cause of argument between the two, and after a particularly nasty altercation, he avoided any mention of his name. He hoped she would ignore the comment.

"You know it's not the same."

Common sense told him to let the topic go, but unwittingly he had become a champion at defending his ex.

"Why not? He was my partner for three years. We lived together for two of those. Or doesn't that count for anything?"

"You know what I mean. Ewan has stepped in as husband, provider, and stepfather. And if you remember, the kids got on fine with Christian. They were always happy to see him. So was Gran."

"But not you."

She exhaled deeply before replying.

"We can't like everyone we meet in this life."

"I rest my case."

"Ewan's genuine," she snapped back, determined to drive home her point. "Not the life and soul of the party perhaps, but he's not a lightweight. He's not the sort to bail on us as soon as times get tough or when something better comes along."

Like Christian. In his mind, Anton filled in the intended last words for her.

"How can you be so sure?"

"Because I know people, and I think I'm a good judge of character," she replied, clearly annoyed with him now. "Just as I saw through Christian, saw him for the liar and manipulator he was. You were so caught up in the whole hero-worship thing you were blind to how much he was using you. Until it was too late."

With the car door pulled open, he stopped and glared at her, a flush warming the skin of his neck. In the few seconds of silence, he considered hurling Ewan's naked performances at her. Instead he took a few deep calming breaths—something he had learned from an ex-colleague who attended yoga lessons—until the moment of irritation had passed. No more parting on bad terms.

Two months after Christian split with him, he had finally found the energy to drive down and stay with Gemma, to seek solace and sympathy from the one person he thought might understand and empathize. In stark contrast, she had been nothing short of brutal, chastising him for wasting time wallowing in self-pity. Still numb from the breakup, he had listened in shocked silence, his face a mask, but inside loathing each of her assertions, especially the claim that Christian had been a conceited and cheating bully who had never been good enough for him. Overnight, with her words stewing and seething inside, he had apportioned to her much of the blame for Christian leaving him. Departing first thing the next morning, their usual twice-weekly calls had ceased for over two months. When finally they resumed—she had been the one to broker the truce—he refused to discuss anything about the visit or Christian, as though neither had happened.

"Me leaving now is about getting back into work," he said softly after a few breaths, because he could not tell her the other more important reason. "Before I am so far removed from what's happening in the legal services market that I become obsolete."

"Don't know why you're so worried. It's only been a few months. Any firm would be lucky to have you," she said, slipping back into her warm, familiar tone and causing a smile to twitch his lips. Since their parents' deaths, Gemma had provided his emotional support, slipping easily into the role of protector.

"Almost six months, Gem. But I appreciate the vote of confidence," said Anton, meeting her eyes again and smiling. Instead of getting in the car, he walked around to her again and pecked her on the cheek. She smelled of buttered pastry and traces of a flowery perfume he hadn't noticed on her before. "I'll give you a call about the house later in the week. And I promise to be back for Christmas, okay? I promise."

"Fine," she huffed in defeat, still not satisfied but kissing him on the cheek before patting the spot with her floury hand. "Call when you get home. Let me know you got back safely."

As he pulled away, leaving her standing alone at the garden gate, guilt filled him, and he almost relented. Instead, turning onto the main road, he floored the accelerator and resolved to ramp up the job search. His sister had enough on her plate without having him to worry about.

Sitting unmoving on the A30, he glanced in the rearview mirror and exhaled a heavy sigh at the line of stationary cars snaking into the distance. How much time would be added to his journey, he had no idea. He loathed uncertainty almost as much as warm beer and television snooker. One thing he knew for sure. If the traffic didn't start moving soon, he'd be too late to meet up with Paul and Julie and, more importantly, miss the off chance that Christian might make an appearance. Maybe that was a good thing.

Eyes squeezed shut, he folded his right arm instinctively across his body and placed the fingers onto his left shoulder, searching for Christian's hand. Christian would rest his hand there even with passengers in the car, even if he had volunteered—usually to Anton's annoyance—to take the backseat behind the driver. Neither had been comfortable or confident enough to hold hands in public, but that one small concession had meant everything. Christian's hands had been large and strong. Even now the memory of the size and warmth of them touching or holding his body made him tremble. But Christian had discovered a new significant other, someone more in touch with his feelings, someone willing to take chances, someone adventurous and equal to the same challenges as Christian. Someone better.

A last minute breakup text from Christian had ended with the words: "You are simply not enough, Anton."

Not telling his sister about drinks with Paul and Julie had been a smart move. She would have seen straight through him. They had been Christian's friends since college. Unlike other of their friends, they had not taken sides after the breakup, had invited Anton to parties and out for group meals—not that he had accepted either—and had even remembered to send him a card on his birthday. After almost letting Julie's call go to voice mail, he picked up at the last minute, maybe to convince himself he was finally getting over Christian. But when she invited him out for a drink with them, suggesting they avoid the Royal Standard because Christian often went there alone on Sunday, Anton had argued that he could handle it, that he had missed his old stomping ground. Hence plans had been laid.

Distant thunder brought him out of his reverie. After fifteen minutes sitting in the motionless car, he decided to switch the engine off. Restless now, he leaned forward and peered through the windscreen. Heavy October clouds filled the air, draining the last of the day's dull light from the sky. Almost on cue, specks of rain spattered onto the glass. Anton threw himself back in his seat and snapped on the wipers. Apart from an occasional car, the opposite lane appeared empty, suggesting that whatever had snagged up the traffic had done so on both sides. A couple of impatient drivers were already performing three-point turns and heading back south.

Ahead of him, through streaks of rain, the Porsche driver pulled the car onto the grass verge and crept forward. About thirty yards farther on, the vehicle disappeared down a country lane. Anton checked the satnav display, but the device indicated no side road. Firing up the engine again and crawling forward toward the taillights of the van, he made up his mind to follow.

As the worsening downpour clattered onto his windscreen, he reached the turnoff in time to witness the Porsche vanishing like a silver bullet around a bend into the narrow lane. If the driver knew a shortcut, Anton would need to keep up. He stomped on the accelerator and plunged into a track dwarfed on either side by tall hedgerows.

"Recalculating route," said the calm female voice of the satnav.

Unlike the main road, the tarmac surface of this one had not been maintained well, and the Audi bumped and bounced along the lane. Heavy rain hammered down from the heavens. Anton flicked on the car's full beam lights and set the wipers clunking furiously. Neither provided any significant improvement to visibility.

"Perform a three-point turn and return to the A30," advised the soft female voice of the satellite navigator.

After a few miles, catching occasional glimpses of the car's scarlet lights glowing in the distance, he reached a crossroads. Almost coming to a stop, he spotted headlights way ahead in the distance, reflecting off the hedgerow. Revving the engine, he thrust the car into gear and roared forward but almost swerved into the wall of a sharp right bend, which took him in a different direction to the other driver.

"Continue on for two miles," said the device.

Despite a flicker of hesitation, Anton continued down the track rather than turning back, even though this wider route ran straight, indicating no turns in the visible distance. On either side, low drystone walling, slick now with rain, replaced the earlier hedgerow, with barren moorland stretching out dim and bleak beyond. Only the car's broad beams of light provided any respite from the heavy rain and darkness.

"Turn right at the next intersection," said the satnav, grabbing Anton's attention.

He began to slow the car, to squint through the thunderous downpour and check for a turning, but there appeared to be nothing obvious in the distance. Once again he hit the gas and hurtled forward, this time passing a remote cottage on his left and narrowly missing a Range Rover parked out front.

"Turn right at the next intersection," said the navigator again.

Just then Anton spotted the rear lights of a car in the distance. He had an instant rush of relief and hammered the old Audi along the lane.

"At the next set of traffic lights, turn right onto Piccadilly Circus," said the voice of the satnav in a strange gargled tone.

"What?" asked Anton, casting an angry glance at the flickering display.

"In ten miles, take exit five off the M26 and follow the signs for Birmingham Airport…." said the strangled voice, cut short as the display blinked, fizzled, and went blank.

"Fine. You've been no bloody help anyway," he muttered, thumping the dormant device with his palm.

Ahead, the lane twisted sharply to the left. Instinctively his foot touched the brake pedal, but as he reached for the accelerator pedal again, the wipers clunked to a halt in the middle of the screen. At the same moment both the headlights and dashboard lights flickered synchronously before failing. Plunged into darkness, Anton steered blindly along the unlit lane. Adrenaline kicked in, and he sucked in a breath before aiming the hurtling beast toward where he thought he had seen a lay-by on the lane's right side. Stamping on the brake pedal, he prayed the car would not collide with anything solid. Forward momentum continued, and the Audi skidded and swerved before the right side dropped into a shallow ditch and slid along a wall with a screech of metal. As the beast came to a sudden, violent halt, engaging the air bags in front, his head slammed against the right-hand doorframe.

With the air bags deflating, bursts of dazzling fireworks illuminated behind his tightly closed eyelids. He remained frozen in his seat, unable to move, his hands clutching the steering wheel and fingers trying to bury themselves into the wheel's plastic molding. Due to the incline of the car, his shoulder dug painfully against the driver's door. When he finally opened his eyes, he exhaled a gasp of breath, holding panic at bay and willing himself to breathe evenly. Rain clattering on the roof and bonnet reverberated throughout the dark interior, filling the sudden silence. Sitting upright as best he could, Anton's vision adjusted gradually to the lack of light and he forced himself to focus his thoughts into action.

First he reached down and twisted the key in the ignition. Dead. Above him, he pushed his fingers at the switch of the internal car light, but again nothing happened. A wave of desperation began to build inside him, tears welling in his eyes, his breaths ragged and threatening hyperventilation.

And then a sudden calm descended on him, warm and intimate, a tranquility tingling through him, as comforting and evocative as submerging in a tub of hot water on a winter's day.

You're not to blame. Some things are beyond our control. You need to move forward now. You still have so much to give. Move forward, Anton.

Like a warm desert breeze, the words floated through and around him.

"RAC," he said aloud, the sound of his voice in the dark adding to his calmness. With relief, he remembered the breakdown service membership card in his wallet and the emergency number programmed into his mobile phone. "Call the RAC."

He unfastened his belt and felt his way awkwardly to the backseat to retrieve the everyday rucksack he used to store his practical items, his lifeline: house keys, mobile phone, digital camera, water bottle, waterproof, small umbrella, and tablet computer. With the bag in his lap, he patted the side where he stored his phone but found an empty pocket. Strange, he thought to himself, he made a ritual of placing the mobile in this handy custom-made holder. After trying the other side and finding the water bottle in its place, he sat back and realized with sudden dismay what he had done. On his rush to leave his sister's house, he had left the damn thing in the charger on the bedside cabinet.

From inside the pack, he yanked out the old tablet computer he had not used all weekend. Welcoming pale light from the device illuminated the car. Within seconds the large digital clock opened on the screen, displaying the time: 19:12. On the off chance, he checked for a wireless Internet connection even though he knew the possibility as remote as his location. Finding nothing, he rested the device in his lap to consider his options.

Even if a public phone box stood somewhere nearby, he had no idea where to look, which would mean searching blindly in the dark. He could stand in the rain and wait in the distant hope of another car coming along, but that might take ages, and with no decent lighting to alert a driver's attention, might also be dangerous. Perhaps, he thought, he should sleep in the car until morning and then get a better idea of his bearings by daylight. The awkward angle of the vehicle would make doing so uncomfortable but not unbearable. To make matters worse, warmth from the heater had already begun to seep away, and apart from his fleece and overcoat, he had nothing to keep him warm. Mentally, however, he filed the idea away as a course of last resort.

With a foot wedged against the driver's door, he clambered across the passenger seat and pushed the car door ajar. Instantly raindrops showered his face, ice cold and sobering. From what he could tell, no lights shone anywhere in the distance, the road swallowed up by the bleakness of moorland.

"Just do *something*," he chastised himself before a crystal clear thought came to him. Hadn't there been a cottage back along the lane with a car outside? That boded well. Surely they would have a telephone? When he made up his mind to run with the idea, his spirits lifted instantly. After throwing the pack out before him, he pushed the door wide and climbed out into the downpour.

CHAPTER 2
GATE-CRASH

AFTER SQUEEZING into his waterproof and pulling on the hood without getting too drenched, he gave the Audi as thorough a check-over as possible. Broken glass crunched underfoot when he trod to the front bumper, but on the driver's side he could discern nothing. Leaned into the ditch and wedged tight against the wall, the entire right wing remained hidden. He locked up, fixed his backpack into place, and trudged off in the direction of the cottage.

Spiteful shards of rain mixed with unwieldy wind stung his eyes and buffeted him from time to time, sending him staggering across the lane like a midnight drunk. By contrast, the elements managed to heighten his senses, chilled air filling his lungs, the rain and forward momentum bringing him back to alert consciousness. Bending into the onslaught, he was surprised at how much he could discern, how fast his eyes grew accustomed to the dark, despite cloud cover and nightfall. With his head down, he trudged forward, following raindrops sparking on the lane's dark surface and using the verge on his left for guidance, looking up to check progress whenever the wind lulled.

After around ten minutes, a glimmer of light twinkled from between the branches of a small tree or bush, and moments later he drew level with the shadowed bulk of the Rover. Without hesitation, he placed his wet palm on the bonnet. Rain may have cooled the metal, but he hoped to detect an echo of warmth from the engine and confirmation of someone at home. Lifeless cold met his touch.

At the front gate he hesitated, appraising the veiled structure. Luminous white paintwork pierced the night and outlined the silhouette of a low stone garden wall. The cottage was long, with two lead-paned windows either side of the front door and five on the upper level. None of them showed any signs of light or life, the only illumination coming from the small one he had spotted earlier at the side of the building. He wondered if anyone could live in such a remote location from day to day. More likely, this was someone's holiday hideaway, a rich city dweller's second home.

A quick glance up and down the empty lane reaffirmed that he had no other choice. With both hands, he shoved at the gate, the hinges giving without a sound, and scrunched the few graveled steps to the front door. A small awning above the portal provided scant shelter from the weather, so Anton left his hood up and patted either side of the shrouded frame for a doorbell. Finding nothing, his hands moved over the door and found a dark lump of metal on the slat between the glass panels. He grabbed hold of the cold knocker and thumped three times in quick succession. After waiting in silence a few moments, accompanied by the hiss and clatter of rain around his feet, he strode forward and performed the routine again. When no sound came from within and no lights sprang to life, a groan of despair escaped him. On impulse he strode along the garden to the first downstairs window and peered inside, but security bars lined the frame and the curtains had been drawn, no evidence of light seeping from the edges. The idea of heading back and resigning himself to sleeping in the car filled him with defeat, but seemed the only option. Unless, he pondered, out of desperation and entirely out of character, he could consider breaking into the house. The mere thought made him nauseated with shame.

Before he had a chance to decide, bright light illuminated the glass panels of the door, and a shadow appeared in one of the frames.

"Who is it?" called the wary voice of a man.

"Hello there," shouted Anton, moving back to the door. "I've had an accident. In my car. Do you have a telephone I can use?"

Through the clatter of rainfall, he heard bolts unlocked and stood facing as the door swung inward. Blinded for a moment by light from the hallway, he blinked into the silhouetted outline of a man.

"Who are you?" asked the man.

"My name's Swann, Anton Swann," said Anton, throwing back his hood despite the heavy rain. "Sorry to disturb, but I didn't know what else to do."

"Good heavens," gasped the man, his features hidden and unreadable.

"Sorry, I must look a bit of a sight. I left my mobile… I mean, I don't have a phone. Otherwise I wouldn't have troubled you," said Anton after a moment's pause. Rain had started to soak his hair, trickle into his eyes and down his cheeks. "If I can just call the RAC, I'll head back and wait by the car, leave you in peace."

"My dear fellow, come inside. You're drenched," said the man, opening the door wide and gesturing Anton to enter the hallway. "And by the way, you're bleeding."

Anton touched the spot where his head had collided with the car frame. Blood covered his fingertips. Once across the threshold, he reached into his pocket for a handkerchief to hold over the throbbing injury. While the man closed and re-bolted the door, Anton felt an instant embrace of central heating and inhaled the faint but unmistakable odor of a roast dinner commingled with the potent scent of musky flowers.

Standing and waiting in silence for the man to finish his task, he peered around the hallway. Soft jazz and deep muffled conversation seeped from behind a closed door at the back of the house. To his right through an open doorway, a room lay in virtual darkness but appeared to be a dining room, with used plates and glasses still sitting on the table. The bright entranceway housed a tasteful arrangement of patterned rugs covering the uneven stone flooring. An oak stairway disappeared upstairs to the right of an antique reception table of polished mahogany, while next to the front door stood an oak coat rack stacked with an assortment of colorful jackets, hats, and umbrellas. Anton grinned to see an old-fashioned black Bakelite telephone sitting pride of place next to a vase of fresh white lilies on the hall table. He also noticed various styles of discarded footwear to one side of the rack.

He assessed the handsome and well-groomed man to be in his early forties. Decked out in warm, comfortable clothes of chocolate baggy cords and matching fleece open at the neck to reveal a mustard polo shirt, he appeared as charismatic and comfortable as his home. For some reason, he would have expected older occupants to inhabit the cottage.

"This is very kind of you," said Anton, standing still on the doormat.

"Nonsense," said the man, pulling open a door beneath the stairwell to reveal a small cupboard. He pulled a pale blue towel from the top of a neat stack and held the item out to Anton. "Here. You're dripping all over the place. Get out of that raincoat and dry yourself off."

Anton did as asked, stuffing the bloodied handkerchief back in his pocket before shrugging off his backpack, removing the waterproof, and unzipping the front of his fleece. As he handed the plastic wrap to the man, he recognized something at the foot of the oak stairwell, where the stone wall housed a large painting. A portrait depicted two young men, one seated and naked, the other bare chested but lying down, both in the full bloom of youth. *The Noonday Heat* by Henry Scott Tuke. He had seen the painting in a collection at an exhibition at the Barbican in London.

"A fan?" asked the man, following Anton's line of vision.

"Very much so," said Anton, wiping his head and face and offering the towel back to the man. Tuke, with his early-twentieth-century depictions of seminaked men, had become a favorite of his, and of the wider gay community. Of course he was also studied and admired by art lovers the world over, irrespective of gender or sexual orientation.

The man studied him for a moment, until Anton began to feel uncomfortable. Suddenly aware of his inaction, he shook his head and seemed to come to life. First of all, he retrieved the towel, on which Anton noted a smear of blood, and afterward spread Anton's damp plastic mac over the umbrella rack.

"Now what do you need? Telephone. Here we are," he said, moving to the phone and lifting the receiver. "She might be a throwback to the fifties, but she works fine."

Anton pulled his wallet from the side pocket of his backpack, then proceeded to remove his plastic RAC membership card. With a nod, he took the telephone from the man and stared at the rotary dial.

"This looks complicated," he said, staring at the numbers and letters in each of the circular holes.

"Give here," said the man with a tut and a chuckle, taking the receiver from him. "I may not understand all the functions my recently acquired mobile telephone can perform, but I know how to operate one of these babies. Let me get you connected, and then I'll go and let the others know what's going on."

Absently wondering what others he could be referring to, Anton read aloud the free phone number and watched as the man hooked his forefinger and dialed. As soon as the line began to ring, he handed the telephone over to Anton. While Anton talked, the man disappeared through the back door. After rattling off his account details with the operator and explaining his predicament, the operator finally asked him to confirm his location. At this point he peered up to see where the man had gone, but found himself still alone. He searched the table for a letter or some sign of an address. Then he asked the operator to hold on, put the receiver onto the table, and was about to head to the back room when the man reappeared.

"They want to know where I am," he said.

"Ah. Yes. We're a bit out in the sticks here. Probably best if I do that rather than try to explain," said the man, picking up the receiver. Anton stood by and listened as the man reeled off a number of A and B roads and a couple of village names Anton had never heard before. Finally, as the man listened to the operator, he peered up and nodded at Anton as though about to hand back the phone, but then stopped and frowned.

"Ninety minutes or so?" said the man, shaking his head at Anton. "You expect him to sit and wait by his car for two hours in this dreadful weather? He's been in an accident, for goodness' sake."

"I don't mind," said Anton, but the man ignored him. On hearing the word "accident," he sensed a trickle of warm blood on his forehead and pulled the handkerchief from his pocket back to his head again.

"Can your recovery person telephone here once they're close by? Perfect, that's settled, then," said the man and proceeded to rattle off a long telephone number. At the end he bid the operator a polite good-bye before replacing the receiver.

Before Anton could say anything, the man said, "It would be negligent of me to send you back out in this weather. You'll catch your death. Now come into the kitchen and make yourself comfortable. Meet the rest of the gang."

Without another word the man led the way toward the room at the back of the cottage, and despite a momentary hesitation, Anton followed. From the next room a voice called out, "Come on, Martin. We were beginning to think you've been abducted."

"Gentlemen. Best behavior, please," said the man called Martin. "We have an unexpected guest."

Anton stepped into the cozy warmth of the room and gazed around at the decor before acknowledging any of those seated. Warmly decorated in a combination of vibrant Portuguese and old English styles, the long kitchen came as an unexpected and pleasurable surprise. Spacious and with sympathetic modernization, the room contained a ten-seater table of rough pine at its heart. Housed in a red brick chimney, an AGA cooker—its cast-iron surrounds of chocolate brown—ran along the left side of the room between two small lead-paned windows. Two large copper pots, one stained with gravy around the rim, sat glistening on the top of the cooker, while a row of various-sized siblings hung from a rail above. On the other side of the room, a rustic Welsh dresser of honeyed pine held rows of Mediterranean patterned plates, cups, and saucers, many of them missing and in use on the table. Without question, this was a working kitchen, the center of the house, not a showroom like others he had seen at friends' and ex-colleagues' trendy houses. Bottles of various wines and port, plates of cold meats, cheese and crackers, a large jug of coffee, and a bowl of fruit filled the table. In the center, the colorful wheel of a Trivial Pursuit board game lay open, although play seemed to have been abandoned or suspended. To complete the homely setting, soft strains of Ella Fitzgerald singing an old jazz ballad came from unseen speakers secreted away among the rafters.

Most of the men seated had turned Anton's way. The man on the left nearest Anton appeared to be the youngest, midtwenties, a little younger than Anton. Beautiful olive-skinned Hispanic features were framed by slicked-back dark hair and bottomless brown eyes. Stripes like chevrons had been carved into the end slope of the left eyebrow, while shiny studs of jet pierced each of his lobes. He wore a burgundy fleece unzipped to the waist with a white singlet beneath, a silver chain culminating in two male "Mars" symbols joined together resting in the dark hair of his muscled chest. When the younger man's eyes followed Anton's gaze down to the pendant, they returned shortly with a knowing wink and a smile. Anton, surprised and embarrassed by this simple familiarity, tore his gaze away and continued to scour the room.

Along from him, the older man in the dark green rugby shirt had begun to remove his arm from the back of the younger one's chair, but then relented. Broad and well defined, he had Gaelic features of freckled skin, red hair, and light stubble. Suggesting the shirt was not simply an accessory, the ridge of his nose had been broken in a couple of places, like the warning sign of a hairpin bend. Anton placed him somewhere in his early thirties and warmed to the playful smile he gave off. Scotsmen had been Christian's thing, and this particular one would have been right on the money.

Of the four men seated, the blond sitting alone at the far end did not appear to have noticed him, his head bowed into his lap, one hand thumbing through a pile of playing cards, the other rubbing a spot on the back of his neck. Where the other men wore warm clothing, he wore a simple, snug-fitting short-sleeved gray T-shirt.

Sitting on the far right of the table, a man around the same age and build as the one called Martin had put down a glass of red wine as Anton entered. Dressed in a similar way to Martin, making casual appear fashionable, he wore wire-framed glasses, and his impeccably groomed auburn hair held less gray than the other man's.

"Everyone, this is—" said Martin before turning to Anton for help. "I'm sorry. What was your name again?"

"Anton Swann," he said, his left hand still clamping the handkerchief to his head. "Had an accident in my car. Down the lane from here. Your friend kindly let me use his telephone."

"God. He looks a bit like—" began the man on the right of the table.

"Gal," said Martin, cutting him off.

"Sorry. Well, as you heard, I'm Gal, short for Gallagher," said the man, standing awkwardly, leaning forward, and holding out his hand in greeting. In the process of shaking hands, the man's gaze wandered to the handkerchief clutched to Anton's head.

"It's nothing," said Anton quietly, shaking his head.

"Sean and Federico," said Martin, indicating the ginger-haired man and the young Spaniard. In unison, the two men smirked and each held a hand up in welcome. "And at the end of the table is Stephen."

Encouraged by the others, Anton held up a hand to the blond, who had finally raised his head. Classically handsome, his face was chiseled, with a slight stubble. In stark contrast to his good looks, a scar cut down the side of his face from brow to cheek. Somewhat unkindly, Anton pictured him as the stereotypical Nazi villain in any number of Second World War movies, minus the uniform and monocle. Enhancing this illusion, the icy glare from his eyes held neither humor nor friendliness but rather irritation at the intrusion. He nodded sharply once in response to Anton's gesture and then carried on sorting through his pack of cards.

"Take a seat," said Gallagher, indicating the pine chair at the opposite end of the table from the blond. "You can probably tell we're at the tail end of a late and rather long and self-indulgent Sunday lunch. It's a tradition. Of sorts."

"Sorry for this. Feel like I'm gate-crashing," said Anton, sitting and realizing for the first time how tired he was.

"Nonsense," said Martin, taking his place next to Gallagher and flashing his friend a knowing look. "We take care of our own."

"Sounds like a lot of crashing for one night," said Sean at the same time, laughing at his own joke. Anton was surprised to hear a playful Irish lilt in the man's voice, not Scottish as he had first assumed. He also noticed the upper molar missing from his smile.

"Not funny," said Federico, nudging his shoulder against the Irishman.

"Were you hurt?" said Stephen from the end of the table, pointing to the handkerchief Anton still clamped to his head.

"A scratch. Banged my head on the doorframe of the car," he said, grimacing.

"Let me take a look," said Stephen, putting down the cards and scraping his chair away from the table.

The words came not so much as an offer but an order, and Anton felt obliged to obey. The blond man stood then, much larger than Anton had imagined, probably three inches taller than Anton's five eleven. Beneath his gray tee he wore baggy black track bottoms and walked barefoot on the flagstones.

"Our resident doctor," said Martin. "Don't worry. You'll be in safe hands. Now, let's get you a coffee and you can tell us your tale of woe."

"In a minute," said Stephen, who had reached Anton's side. "Let me check him over first."

Anton pulled the handkerchief away, but instead of looking at his wound, the man knelt down, put his large, cold hands firmly either side of Anton's face, and turned his head toward him. With knotted brows, his slate blue eyes flicked back and forth between Anton's. Anton could not stop his own from tracing the scar on the man's face.

"How do you feel now?" he asked. "Any nausea or dizziness?"

"I don't think so," said Anton, although embarrassment had started to leak into his cheeks.

"You either have or you haven't," said the man. "It's not a difficult question."

"Then no," said Anton, absolutely sure he had begun to blush.

"Your pupils aren't dilated, which is a good sign," he said, his breath scented with sweet wine. "Now let me check your wound. Sean, get me the first aid kit from the drawer behind you."

With Stephen busy cleaning and dressing the wound, Anton accepted coffee from Martin and wrapped his cold hands around the mug. Without moving his head too much, he tilted the hot mug to his lips to take a couple of refreshing sips. In response to the silence in the room and in order to take his mind off the man standing over him, he began telling his tale of misfortune.

"Happened on the drive home from Newquay back to Croydon. I was attending my grandmother's funeral this weekend," he began, accompanied by murmured condolences.

"Not dressed like that, I hope," muttered the voice above him.

"Stupid, really," said Anton, ignoring the remark. "There was a snarl-up on the A30, and this Porsche in front of me dipped out and pulled onto a side road. I thought he might know a shortcut, so decided to follow. But my old Audi's no match for a Porsche, and I got lost. Then, chasing him down the lane from here, the electrics on my car failed completely and I ended up in a ditch."

"Jackpot. Hawk's Tor jinx," said Sean, holding up the palm of one hand and addressing his comments to Martin. "What more proof do you need?"

"Lord, not that old chestnut again?" said Martin, raising his eyes to the heavens.

"Sean reckons there's some sort of curse in the area," said Gallagher, smirking at Anton. "Do you think you were cursed, Anton?"

Stephen snorted softly while rubbing a pungent ointment into Anton's wound that stung and made his eyes smart. Anton began to turn toward Gallagher, but Stephen yanked his head back.

"Hold still."

"I didn't use the word curse," said Sean, "but ask any of the locals in the village. They call it the Hawk's Tor Phenomenon. Something to do with ancient ley lines intersecting. It's why electrical equipment fails from time to time. Why do you think you can never get a signal on your mobile phone?"

"The answer to that, my dear friend, is far more scientific," said Martin. "The cottage is in a dead zone. Sitting in a valley surrounded by hills. Signals from the provider's antennae are blocked. Ten minutes' drive down the lane and you can call anywhere in the world."

"Is that why my watch stops every time I come here? Or why the house lights gave us a merry show the last time we visited?" asked Sean.

"I thought you'd attributed the lights to the resident ghost nobody's ever seen," said Martin, a playful smile on his face and a wink at Anton.

"You have to forgive Sean," said Gallagher, directly to Anton. "He's from the mystical Emerald Isles, the land of the leprechaun."

"And insists on buying cheap watches," added Martin, making everyone around the table laugh.

"Feck the lot of you," said Sean, laughing too and then taking a swig of wine. "You know I'm right."

"What do you do?" Federico asked Anton. He probably did so in an effort to change the conversation. "I mean, for work."

"I'm a solicitor," said Anton. "I worked in one of the big city firms for six years. Mainly corporate law, mergers and acquisitions, initial public offerings, that kind of thing. But I got laid off six months ago. Thanks to the global economic downturn, I'm currently between jobs."

"Unemployed, then," said the man hovering over him, pressing a bandage onto his head.

"Yes, I suppose," said Anton.

"No suppose about it. If you don't have work," said the man, "then you're unemployed."

The comment prickled. He had put in his time—years at university—achieving a first in his law degree and finally winning a coveted trainee contract in a major city firm, sweating his backside off for two years before qualifying as a solicitor. Surely he could call himself a solicitor even if he wasn't currently practicing. He decided to let the jibe go.

"Okay, you're all fixed up," said Stephen, replacing the first aid kit in the drawer on the way back to his seat. "No stitches, but you'll have a nasty bump come morning."

"You should eat something," said Federico, leaning into Anton.

"I'm fine, thanks. The coffee's delicious, though," he said, raising the mug to his lips. Assortments of meats lay on a plate nearby, and he realized he hadn't eaten since lunchtime, but he had no appetite. In fact, the thought of eating anything made him queasy. When he raised his eyes, he was relieved to hear the topic of conversation had moved on. Despite appreciating their hospitality, part of him wanted the telephone to ring so that he could be on his way, even though there was no chance of meeting up with Paul and Julie now.

At the far end of the table, Stephen and Gallagher discussed some trip abroad or another, while Sean had now engaged Federico in a whispered conversation. Relaxing in his seat, Anton allowed the hubbub and the congeniality to wash over him.

"So you practice law? Surely not by choice?" asked Martin, a playful arc to his left eyebrow.

Anton smiled. He liked the host, liked his calming tone and his gentle sense of humor.

"Actually, yes. My father was in the profession, so let's say I felt a duty to follow," said Anton, but mentioned nothing about the fact that his mother and father had died long before they had the chance to see him qualify. "How about you?"

"We run a couple of antique shops in Oxford. At least I do. Gal helps out when he has the time. He still has his high-powered job, which helps to finance our other ventures, the shops and an import-export business," said Martin, nodding at the Welsh dresser. "Over there's one our pieces."

Anton turned and gave the kitchen a fresh appraisal, his eyes coming to rest on the piece of furniture Martin had pointed out.

"I admire how you've modernized but still maintained the integrity of the place," said Anton. "You know, combining subtle structural changes and up-to-date appliances, but all done without losing any of the kitchen's original charm. The Aga, the dresser, and the Bakelite phone are such character pieces. And the Henry Tuke at the foot of the stairs is an absolute delight, perfectly complements the rusticity."

"Actually—" began Martin.

"*My* Tuke," said Stephen, leaning forward and interrupting. "*My* phone, *my* kitchen. You're in *my* cottage."

"I'm sorry," began Anton, turning confused to Martin. "I thought—"

"What? Because Martin answered the door, you assumed—" said Stephen.

"Well, yes," said Anton, this time frowning and cutting him off. His sensed his cheeks flushing scarlet. He had no idea why the doctor had taken such a dislike to him. Not everyone he met warmed to his admission to being in the legal profession, but this man hadn't even known that until a few moments ago.

"Surely they teach you lawyers about the dangers of making assumptions?" said Stephen, glaring directly at Anton.

You lawyers? This time Anton held his ground.

"They do. But as you insisted on correctly pointing out, I'm no longer a solicitor," he said, fixing a smile in place. "I'm unemployed."

Next to him, Federico snorted softly into his fist. Anton thought he saw a glimmer of a smirk flash across the doctor's lips. He wondered if the man was trying to humiliate him on purpose.

"Stephen," said Gallagher in a mildly admonishing tone, leaning over and patting the doctor's arm. "Give the poor fellow a break. He's been through enough for one night."

Once again conversations started up around him, but this time he allowed Martin to do the talking without interrupting or being tempted to make any more observations, simply nodded to demonstrate his understanding. Peripherally, he sensed the doctor staring at him from time to time but made a point of not making eye contact.

"This song is lovely, haunting. Who's this singer?" asked Gallagher during a lull in conversation around the table. "I love the voice."

"No idea," said Sean, reaching for the pile of CD covers behind him. "Isn't this one of yours, Stephen?"

"Not mine. This belonged to—" said Stephen, appearing to catch himself. "One from an old jazz compilation. But I can't for the life of me remember the name of the singer."

Something struck Anton as odd in the way they all fell silent, listening politely. Anton stared down at the table and did the same. He knew both singer and song: Mimi Perrin singing *Naima,* written by John Coltrane. His father's collection contained the same recording, one of a pile of old LPs that had become Anton's. Knowledge he decided to keep to himself.

"The trivial game," said Federico, coming to life and breaking the silence. "Before Anton arrived. Let's continue."

"Trivia. And you hate the game," murmured Sean, giving Federico a quizzical look.

"Yes, but we have an extra player now," said Federico, kissing Sean on the cheek and then turning to Anton. "You are on our side, by the way."

"You really want to?" said Stephen. "It's late."

"It's a version of Trivial Pursuit that Martin found. One adapted from the original," said Sean, leaning forward and addressing Anton. "This one is based on arty-farty subjects and literature questions. That kind of shite. Hope you're good. Marty and Gal are wiping their backsides with us."

"Not sure I'll be much help," said Anton. He hated trivia games.

"No spectators. You'll be on our team. Three against two. Stephen's the referee because he's the host. If you do not know any answers, don't worry, Anton. You will be in good company," said Federico, leaning across to Stephen and taking the cards. "Their team had just landed on orange when you knocked. Classical literature."

"I thought orange was sports," said Anton.

"Not in this version," said Sean with a huff. "If it was, we'd be the ones wiping the floor with them."

Sean took a card from the top of the pack. He scanned the surface a couple of times before beginning to recite.

"Name of the book by a famous French author with the first sentence: 'For a long time, I went to bed early.'"

Anton had no idea of the writer, but he warmed to the simplicity of the line, which resembled his own life of late.

"You have any idea?" whispered Federico to Anton after a moment's pause.

Anton shook his head. The room had become noticeably hotter. He took a couple of sips of lukewarm coffee, which had acquired a bitter, metallic taste.

"Come on, then, Marty," said Sean. "I can see by your smug grin you know the answer."

"The first line of Marcel Proust's *À La Recherche du Temps Perdu*," said Martin, in the midst of topping up his glass of red wine. "In fairness, I studied French literature in high school."

"Followed by civil engineering at uni. Neither particularly helpful in the shop," said Gallagher, pulling a face while retrieving the card from Sean and sliding the rest to the middle of the table.

"Not to rub it in, but that also means our team has a full complement of segments to your one," said Martin as Gallagher popped an orange piece into their container. "If we make the center and answer correctly, we win. And you do the dishes."

"As you can probably tell," murmured Sean, addressing Anton again while Gallagher threw two fours and overshot the finishing post. "We only play this stupid game to make the old men around the table feel important and intelligent."

Martin winked at Anton while Federico threw enough to land them on a blue spot, classical poetry. Martin picked a card from the pile, then squinted and frowned at the words.

"Beginning lines of a sonnet. So this one officially eludes me," he said, citing directly from the card. "Name of the poet. *Though shadows may cross our lives without permission, also spirits there are that make us sing. Listen to their voices. And let their beauty ignite you.*"

"My God. So beautiful," whispered Anton. Embarrassed at having spoken aloud without thinking, he peered up nervously and caught Stephen staring at him.

"This I do not believe," squealed Federico, flinging an arm around Sean. "Finally one I know, except the words sound much better spoken in their original language. Spanish. Antonio Carlos. From Sonnet of Forgiveness."

"You are one brilliant man," said Sean, standing up and pecking a kiss on Federico's cheek. "Now if you'll forgive me, I need to visit the little boy's room to relieve the complaint in my bowels."

"Another slice to Sean's team," said Martin, shuffling the cards and pushing them across the table while Sean disappeared into a small room off the back of the kitchen.

A few turns later, Martin finally managed to get their playing piece onto the board's center hexagon. In Sean's absence, Federico called for them to answer on American literature.

"Ah," said Federico, drawing a card from the pack and handing it to Anton. "Some of these English words are difficult for me. Do you mind?"

Anton took the card from Federico, and the younger man went to the porcelain sink to fill his tumbler with water. As Anton began to scan the words, his vision became unfocused.

"I—I can't read this," he said softly. The words on the card would not stay still but blurred and bulged no matter how hard he stared at them.

"Need my glasses?" said Gallagher with a soft chuckle. Anton also heard the sound of a chair scraping on the stone floor.

"No. But I think I might be going to—" he began but stopped as blood drained from his face and a tidal wave of nausea rocked him. He stood quickly from his seat but then caught his footing in the chair legs and began to fall sideways. Desperately, he tried to grab the edge of the table as he went down, in time to see the outline of a hazy form coming toward him.

"I've got you."

Stephen's words and a sharp ringing were the last sounds he heard as the lights in the kitchen drained away. Strong arms caught his shoulders, stopping him from crashing onto the stone floor.

CHAPTER 3
ENCOUNTERS

ANTON SURFACED from a swarm of black and gray specters into pale lamplight. Christian had been there, calling his name, reaching one strong arm around his shoulders and the other beneath his knees, lifting him up to the safety of a mountain ledge. Now a powerful odor ravaged his nose and stung his eyes, a pungent chemical smell he could not place. Laid out on a cushioned surface, his head propped up by soft pillows, he croaked out a moan of complaint. As he blinked open his eyes, a blurry silhouette hovered over his face, holding something beneath his nose. He pushed the offending hand away.

"He will be okay?" came the accented voice of a figure from the end of the bed, someone in the process of pulling off a shoe from Anton's left foot. The other one had already been removed. Somebody had also placed a warm woolen blanket over his torso.

"What happened?" said Anton, his voice a gravelly rasp.

"Delayed concussion," said the closer voice—not Christian's, but one he had heard before somewhere. The man sat on the side of the bed and screwed the lid onto a small bottle. "You've been out for around ten minutes. Should have kept a better eye on you."

"Shall I stay?" said the voice across the room.

"No need, Rico. Go help Sean and Gal in the kitchen. Get them to load up the dishwasher," said the man.

After the other figure had left, the man bent down to collect something from the floor.

"Where am I?"

"Safe," said the voice, calm but brusque. A sound of Velcro being ripped open came from his right. When a hand grabbed his wrist and tried to place something over it, Anton pulled his arm away.

31

"You're in the spare bedroom. Now hold still. I need to take your blood pressure," said the voice, the hand reaching for Anton's wrist again.

"Leave me the fuck alone," said Anton, yanking the hand away again and trying to sit up. Pain screamed across his temple, and he released a cry of anguish, tears squeezing from his eyes. Falling back down, he fingered his forehead and found a bandage there. "Who are you? And where's Christian?"

"Anton," said the voice, this time concern filtering into the tone. "Do you remember what happened? How you got here?"

"How do you know my name?"

"Try to think back," said the man. "You were driving home from Newquay. You took a shortcut and had an accident. That's how you ended up here."

In spite of the throbbing ache in his head, he concentrated his mind back to the evening, to earlier events. A memory seeped back into focus of speed and rain and darkness. And then a later one of grateful warmth and of being an uninvited addition to the tail end of an all-male dinner party. This man was Stephen, the doctor.

"Shit. I crashed my car," he said and then sat upright, causing another bolt of agony to come pounding into his head. "The recovery service—?"

"Is being taken care of right now. By Martin," said Stephen, placing his hands on both shoulders and gently easing him back down. Afterward he slipped the sleeve of the blood pressure device over Anton's arm. "He had to take your car keys, in case you wonder where they are. Said he'll let you know more later, but they'll probably have to tow your car to a local garage. Right now you need to rest. You're under my care and supervision."

Pressure around his upper arm tightened as the band inflated, while the doctor sitting next to Anton observed.

"If you could let me have the number of a taxi service," he said as the tightening stopped and the beeping sound continued, "or a local hotel, I could be out of your hair."

"You're not listening," muttered Stephen, his eyes glued to the monitor's display. "I need to keep you under observation. You're not going anywhere tonight."

Anton felt as though he should protest, but also knew he was not strong or stable enough to move unaided. Despite feeling disorientated, he was also annoyed and ashamed. If he had only listened to his sister and stayed on a few days, none of this would have happened. With no other choice, he began to relax and let the doctor do his work.

"I thought about sleeping in the car, you know. Waiting until morning," said Anton as the monitor gave a long final beep.

"And imagine how that might have turned out," said Stephen, curt again, ripping open the Velcro sleeve. "As expected, your blood pressure's on the low side. Take these pills with some water, and then try to get some sleep. If you feel unwell during the night, press the button on this device."

He indicated a small white gadget like a walkie-talkie on the bedside cabinet. Christian's grandfather had sold a range of the devices.

"Is that—?"

"A baby monitor," said Stephen with a gentle snort of amusement. "My sister leaves one here for when she visits with her brood. It's not switched to listen in, but if you press the button on the side, an alert will sound and a light will illuminate on the one in my room."

"What if you're asleep?"

"I won't be. Now before I go, take your medication."

Anton reached for the pills and glass of water beneath the bedside lamp and dutifully washed everything down. Satisfied, Stephen bent down beside the bed to collect whatever he had set there and then began to walk toward the door.

"Look. Stephen, isn't it?" said Anton. "Thank you for everything. I'm sorry I messed up your evening. But I didn't know what else to do. What I am trying to say, in my less than eloquent way, is that I really do appreciate—"

"Not necessary," said the doctor, who had hesitated at the door before turning back. "Truth is, I think they all rather enjoyed the drama. Made a traditionally entertaining get-together even more memorable. Now get some rest."

Left alone and fighting his tiredness, Anton took in the lamplit room. Various sizes of suitcases had been pushed against one wall, next to a pile of boxes. White netted curtain covered the one window, nothing more substantial. First light would be sure to wake him. Replacing the smelling salts came an odor he recognized well from the unused rooms in his grandmother's house, the powdery scent of dust and neglect. Apart from the bed and bedside cabinet, an old desk of heavy oak and matching swivel chair were the only other items of furniture.

From downstairs came distant voices murmuring indistinguishable words, probably discussing the health of their unwanted guest. Anton sighed, defeated. He reached for the lamp switch and extinguished the light. Sometimes, he thought as sleep sucked him under, you simply have to give in to whatever fate throws your way.

As though surfacing from a deep lake, he gasped awake in the night. Taking a deep breath, he lay unmoving, staring at the dark ceiling, listening to the sounds of the cottage. Apart from constant rain spattering against the windowpane, the house remained silent. Christian had been there again in his dreams, his dark curly locks and handsome features looking down from his vantage point on a rock ledge and daring Anton to climb the steep cliff and join him. Anton had felt the familiar, ragged fear of heights consume him and hesitated too long. This had invoked a curt rebuke from Christian and a disgusted shake of his head before he had set off up the rock face alone. From below, Anton watched powerless as his ex-lover climbed away into the clouds.

Carefully he lifted his head from the pillow and immediately froze. The ghostly outline of a man stood at the window observing him, a hand holding a cigarette moving slowly toward his mouth and stopping. As he watched, the end of the cigarette burned brightly. His heart racing, Anton fumbled for the switch on the bedside lamp. In the dull light he spun around, but nobody stood there, only the net curtains, snagged together in the breeze where the window had been opened a crack. He swung his legs over the bed, stood up gradually, and remained unmoving for a moment to get a sense of his stability. Satisfied, he walked to the window. Scarlet lights trailed across the night sky, the sight of a distant passenger jet sending a shiver though him.

Leaning his head against the cool window frame, he checked his watch: three forty-five. A painful twinge in his bladder told him he would need the bathroom soon. Comforted at feeling better but anxious that he had no idea where to find the toilet in the unfamiliar dwelling, he opened the door and stepped out into the corridor. To his left, soft light from a small brass lamp set on a semicircular hall table illuminated the area around the top of the stairs. Beyond that, the corridor lay in darkness. All visible doors looked identical. Then he recalled the Irishman, Sean, using a restroom at the back of the kitchen. Perhaps, he thought, he could slip downstairs without waking anyone. Stepping out onto the hallway carpet, he made his way quietly toward the stairs, random floorboards complaining as his foot touched them. As he passed the door on his right, he heard soft snoring from within and crept farther forward. At the top of the stairs, he could see better into the other wing of the cottage. On the right, at the far end of the corridor, a glow filtered from beneath a door. He wondered if someone had left the bathroom light on for him. Stealing farther along the hall, he passed another room on his left from which he also heard soft snuffling sounds. When he reached the last door, he started to grab the handle but then hesitated. As a precaution, he brought his hand up and, using the knuckle of his forefinger, rapped softly on the door.

"Yes?" came Stephen's voice. "Who is it?"

Anton muttered a curse. He wanted to turn and head back to the stairs, but to do so now would appear rude or ridiculous. Instead he took a deep breath and turned the Bakelite door handle.

Inside the large bedroom, Stephen sat on top of the cover of a king sized bed, still in the same tee and sweats, reading a thick paperback. He turned to Anton as the door opened.

"Sorry," said Anton, his hand still on the handle. "Trying to find the bathroom. Saw the light and thought this must be the one."

"Other end of the corridor. Come out of your room and turn right, same side," said Stephen. He looked tired, but his voice showed no signs of sleep. The baby monitor's twin brother lay on his bedside cabinet.

"Thanks," he said, relieved and about to close the door.

"How are you feeling?" said Stephen, placing his book facedown on the bed and folding his arms across his chest.

"Better. Much better, thanks," said Anton. "Not sure what was in those pills, but they knocked me out."

"I doubt that," said Stephen. "They were common, off-the-shelf paracetamol, nothing more. You were just tired. A body induces sleep to help self-repair."

"Something did the trick," said Anton and then signaled the corridor with his thumb. "Anyway, I'd better...."

"I've got an en suite," said Stephen, indicating a door at the back of his bedroom. "Be my guest. Pull the cord for the light. Inside left."

Anton hesitated a moment before nodding his thanks and walking to the entrance. On yanking the cord, dazzling fluorescent light flooded the bathroom. He shut the door and headed straight for the toilet. As soon as he had lifted the seat and begun to relieve himself, he took in the room's extravagance. Where the kitchen had been restyled with all the original cottage features in mind, the bathroom had been entirely modernized in porcelain, marble, and chrome. The huge Victorian style bathtub stood on cast-iron lion's feet, while a large shower area had been separated from the room by a full-length door of smoked glass, a huge stainless steel showerhead the size of a manhole cover hanging from the ceiling. Next to where he stood, two hand basins of smoked glass sat atop the white marble surface, and mirrored under-lit cabinets lined the wall.

He finished off and then ran his hands beneath cold water from the tap, splashing some onto his face, the sensation at the same time bracing and refreshing. Feeling awake now, he checked himself in the cabinet's mirror and saw the plaster on his head. He hadn't realized Stephen had cut a clump of hair away to make the plaster stick, leaving behind a tiny bald spot. Apart from that, he looked well enough, perhaps a slight bruising beneath each eye from lack of sleep but nothing more.

With uncharacteristic curiosity, he gently plucked open the door of the cabinet and smiled to see many of the same brands of products he used. Stephen, by contrast, kept six or more of each common item: tubes of toothpaste, bottles of amber mouthwash, containers of liquid soap. Anton assumed he did so because of the cottage's remote location. Opening the right-hand door, the sight could not have been more different. Filled from top to bottom with boxes and bottles of prescription medicines, the names of which he had never heard, and other medical items such as bandages, syringes, antiseptic wipes, and gauze, the cupboard resembled the shelves of a chemist, except that some of these items appeared to have been used. As he closed the door, Anton could only think the doctor kept his own supply of medicines to hand in case of any local emergencies.

He wiped his hands on a plump white cotton towel and, as he exited, snapped off the light. Stephen still sat upright on the bed, reading his book again, but registered Anton as soon as he entered.

"That was an unexpected surprise," said Anton, closing the bathroom door.

Stephen frowned, puzzled, lowering the paperback.

"The bathroom," clarified Anton. "I thought I'd find some early twentieth century plumbing disaster, only to discover five star luxury."

Stephen nodded but remained unsmiling.

"I'll let you get back to your book," said Anton, deflated, and began to walk toward the door.

"So much time and money spent on this place," said Stephen, taking in the room. His voice changed, became serious and sad. "Taught me an important lesson. If you run out of money, there are always ways to find more. But if you run out of time…."

Anton nodded sagely, even though he had no idea what the man meant or how to respond. But then neither did it feel right to leave him alone. After an awkward pause, and in an effort to make conversation, he said, "Don't you ever get tired?"

Stephen spun to face him, a mix of hurt and sorrow in his face. Anton's heart leaped, but he struggled quickly to clarify.

"I mean, it's four o'clock in the morning," he said, tapping his wristwatch. "And you're still awake."

Slowly Stephen's features softened.

"I don't sleep," he said, then added, "Not much, anyway. Couple of hours, tops. Doctor's syndrome."

"You want some company?" asked Anton, standing awkwardly in the room. As soon as the words were out he regretted them, but he followed through so Stephen would not notice his hesitation. "I'm not really tired either. Could make some tea if you want, as long as I can figure out where to find everything."

Stephen scrutinized him so long and hard that Anton began to feel uncomfortable.

"Go and rest," said Stephen dismissively, returning his attention to the book.

After Anton had stepped out and closed the door behind him, he leaned against the frame for a moment to breathe. As he headed toward the landing, a silhouetted figure from the opposite end approached him, from what Anton assumed to be the hallway bathroom.

"Anton?" the figure called in a hushed whisper.

As he entered the light from the hall lamp, he could see the person was Federico. Unashamedly naked, his tanned body sauntered forward, the young athletic chest and thighs matted with dark curly hair, his not insubstantial cock nestled in a mound of the same, bouncing off either thigh as he drew closer. He stopped before Anton and placed a hand on his shoulder.

"Were you in Stephen's room?" he said in hushed tones. An eyebrow arched over one of his beautiful sleep-fuddled eyes. Sometime during the night, the neat, slicked-back midnight hair that Anton had admired so much in the kitchen had taken on a bushfire life of its own.

"I saw the light on. Thought it was the bathroom," Anton replied, matching the Spaniard's tone.

"Ah," said Federico. "And did he tell you to fuck off?"

Anton snorted softly.

"Something like that."

"Don't let him bother you, my friend," said Federico. "He didn't like me either when we first met. But Sean says he has known a lot of pain in his life. And what is it you English call this type of person? Ah yes, damaged goods. He is damaged goods."

Damaged goods. Anton had overheard one of Christian's friends calling him the same thing after their breakup. He knew all about damaged goods. Did that explain Stephen's hostility? Someone had dumped him, so he had decided to take his resentment out on the rest of the world.

"Thanks for the advice," said Anton, preparing to go. But Federico was not finished with him.

"So what is your story?" he asked with a slight shove from the hand still on his shoulder. "You have anyone special?"

"Not at the moment."

"But you did."

"Yes."

"Girlfriend or boyfriend?"

"What do you think?" said Anton, looking him straight in the eyes, a little rattled by the quick-fire interrogation.

"And why do you split up?"

"Because he met someone else."

"Hah! I knew it," said Federico, squeezing Anton's shoulder. "So when is the last time you have sex?"

"What?" said Anton, stifling a laugh. "None of your business."

"Long time, then," said Federico. "So you want come have threesome with Sean and me? He thinks you are hot. We both do."

"As tempting as your offer sounds," said Anton, removing Federico's hand from his shoulder and slipping past him. "I'm still convalescing."

"Take more chances, Anton," chided the Spaniard. "You may find you enjoy yourself."

"See you in the morning," said Anton, watching from his bedroom door as Federico's tight bronzed buttocks disappeared into the shadows. If not for the accent, he mused, those could have been Christian's words of advice.

"Maybe not," called Federico, a shadowy outline turning in the doorway to his room. "Sean and me, we need to leave early. But hope to meet you again soon. Maybe we can hook up in London. We get down there quite often. And I have a friend you will like."

"I'd like that," said Anton, even though he thought the chances highly unlikely.

Secure in the room, he lay down on the bed and stared at the ceiling, feeling sure he would not be able to sleep again. Seeing Federico in the hallway, beautiful and naked, had stirred up feelings of longing. He closed his eyes, his cock springing to life and straining against his jeans while his fertile imagination began to assemble a fantasy with Anton nestled between the two men. Not for the first time, he reminded himself that he had been out of the game for far too long.

CHAPTER 4
HIKE

A CAR engine starting up and driving away from the cottage woke him to a new day, one with the bonus of sunlight flooding the bedroom. When he leaned forward, he noticed the luggage he had taken to his sister's had been placed in the room against the wall, his black suit carrier draped across the top. Someone had retrieved them from the backseat before they towed the car away. Was it the same someone who had been in the bedroom during the morning while he slept? Still in the clothes he had worn the day before, he was grateful for the chance to be able to change into something fresh. Whenever he traveled, he had a habit of overpacking, something he had picked up from attending one-day business meetings or negotiations in Paris or Brussels that could easily turn into two- or three-day marathons, so he knew there would be a full change of clothing. When he rolled over in the bed, away from the daylight, he only meant to drowse for a few moments.

Someone tapping on the bedroom door woke him some time later. Without waiting for a response, Martin entered. Dressed for the weather, he sported a thick sweater of moss green and black jeans. In his hands he held a small tray, and he had a plump white bath towel thrown over his shoulder.

"Morning, sleepyhead," he said. "It's after nine thirty. Thought you might like some tea. Not sure how you take it, so there's milk and sugar on the side. And of course, your medicine."

Anton carefully pulled himself into a sitting position as Martin rested the tray on the bedside cabinet and then perched himself on the edge of the bed.

"First-class medical attention and now room service," said Anton, relieved to feel no nausea. "When do I get the bill?"

Martin laughed. "Strict instructions. 'Keep an eye on him. And don't let him go anywhere until I'm back.'"

"Stephen?" asked Anton.

"He's driving Sean and Rico to Plymouth station. Then he's off to the hospital for his morning appointments," said Martin. "Should be back around two or three."

"Who brought my things from the car?" asked Anton, nodding across the room.

"I did. Stephen dropped them in for you while you were sleeping," said Martin, his features becoming serious. "And now about your car, Anton. My goodness, you were very lucky not to have been more seriously injured. Frankly, I was shocked when I saw the damage. Front axle broken. And the impact smashed in most of the right wing. They've towed the poor beast into Launceston for inspection, but the service man kept muttering something about it being a certified write-off."

"I see," said Anton, his heart sinking even though he had expected as much. His years with the Audi had been good ones, the vehicle one of the most reliable he had ever driven. And now, to add insult to injury, not only did he have no job and no boyfriend, he also had no car.

"The good news, he told me, is you had the common sense to purchase a decent fully comprehensive car insurance through them. So they've given me the telephone number of the Launceston garage, and as long as you call before four o'clock, they'll arrange to have a hire car delivered here. Part of your cover."

"I hadn't even thought of that," said Anton, suddenly overwhelmed by the generosity and concern of these strangers. "Martin, I don't know what to say."

"You don't need to say anything," said Martin, winking and pulling the towel from his shoulder. "As I told you yesterday, we look after our own. Now drink your tea before it gets cold. Stephen made breakfast and had the sense to put some to one side for you, away from Federico's greedy gaze. But you'll probably want to shower and change first. I gather you figured out where the bathroom is during the night. Today we've been given custody of the patient. Stephen said you should really rest all day, but it's such a lovely morning that we managed to persuade him to let us take you on a short hike—more of a stroll really—across the moors for some bracing fresh air followed by a pub lunch. He agreed as long as you let us know how you're feeling, if you get tired or feel unwell at all. We know just the place. Head down to the kitchen when you're dressed and ready. Is there anyone you need to call? To let them know where you are?"

"I suppose I ought to phone my sister," he replied, the burning in his cheeks on processing the remark about finding the bathroom not subsiding. He supposed Stephen had told them all at breakfast about their uninvited guest stumbling into his bedroom during the night. "But I can do so later."

By eleven, after a much-needed breakfast of strong tea and freshly squeezed orange juice with scrambled egg and smoked salmon on toast, Anton stood across the road from the cottage with Martin, waiting for Gallagher to lock up. Shaved, showered, and dressed in clean, warm clothing, including a pair of green Wellington boots Martin had found in a shoe closet and that fit him perfectly, Anton felt ready for the outdoors. Expecting to feel a little unsure on his feet from the effects of the night before, he instead felt solid and anxious to get moving. Martin and Gallagher looked the part, decked out in matching green Barbour jackets and hiking boots, denims tucked in at the ankle to thick woolen socks. From a distance, the two of them could easily have been mistaken for brothers—or bookends.

In the clear light of morning, he had a good view of the long cottage, maintained and renovated as faithfully as the interior. Slate roof tiles glistened in the sunshine, a testament to a night of rain, culminating in squat stone brick chimneys at the near and far ends. Plain wooden window boxes, currently vacant and rain stained, underlined the downstairs windows, and only hardy evergreen shrubs poked above the dry stone wall encasing the front garden. In the morning light, the racing-green front door shone glossy and homely, the bronze lion's head knocker sitting pride of place in the middle. Only the small downstairs windows, metal barred and sparsely curtained in cream fabric, appeared vaguely unwelcoming. Nevertheless the property of white facade and black woodwork radiated a very agreeable old world charm.

"Used to be a real coach house," said Martin, seeing Anton scan the building and coming to stand next to him. "Built around 1735, a stop-off point between London and the Cornish coastline. Before the renovations, there were nine small bedrooms on the first floor. Now there are five and a small study. You probably didn't get a chance to see, but there are also stables out the back. Here stands a little piece of history."

"How did Stephen come by the place?" asked Anton.

"His father has quite a portfolio of properties," said Martin. "Bought in the seventies, I believe. Used to rent this one out as a holiday home. He decided to offload a couple of them, including this one, when he retired and the maintenance and repairs got too much. Stephen stepped in and asked if he could buy the place. His father signed the deeds over but wouldn't take a penny. Just as well. I helped with the furnishings—that's why I know my way around the place—but the renovations alone cost a small fortune."

"A listed property?" asked Anton.

"Grade II, which caused a few problems with plans for the overhaul. Thank goodness Stephen's father still has some influence over at the local authority planning department."

"And Stephen lives here alone?" asked Anton.

"He does now," said Martin, turning away.

Gallagher had brought a walking stick with him and pointed toward a turnstile farther down the lane. Regular visitors to the area, the men knew the terrain well, and before long they were tracing the gentle slope of a narrow path. Overnight rainwater had created large pools in and around the muddy tracks, and Anton's borrowed boots turned out to be a savior. Sploshing through the middle while the two men carefully skirted them, Anton felt a welcome sense of fun and freedom. Within fifteen minutes they had scaled the top of a hillock of coarse grass and stopped for a breather. Already Anton felt alive, more substantial, blood moving through his body. From their vantage point, they overlooked a sea of rolling moorland in each direction, but now the coach house was lost from view.

"We hear you bumped into Rico last night," said Gallagher as they followed Martin, walking together down the far side of the hill. So, thought Anton, the young Spaniard had told them all about their chance nocturnal encounter.

"Naked as a baby," said Anton, avoiding any mention of stumbling into Stephen's bedroom. "He invited me to their room for a threesome."

Ahead and eavesdropping on the conversation, Martin roared with laughter. After managing to catch his breath, he called back, "And did you?"

"If I had, I'm sure you would have heard all about it by now," said Anton, tilting his head to a grinning Gallagher.

"And he tells us you're currently on the market" came Martin's voice.

Anton shook his head, trying to keep the embarrassment from his face. Federico had dished the whole sordid conversation.

"Taking time off for good behavior," he replied, nodding to Gallagher, an expression of mock seriousness.

"Don't wait too long," called Martin. "You're a good looking lad, but we all come with a shelf life. And the older we get, the fussier we become."

Gallagher rolled his eyes at Anton and leaned in toward him.

"Old married couples," he whispered. "We're always looking to marry off the youngsters."

Martin led them confidently along a muddy path bordered by puddles that meandered around a medium-sized mound. Only then did he realize Martin was picking an easier route to avoid the exertion of any steep hills. Anton had seen no other hikers, but as they rounded the hill, a black Labrador came rushing up to them, panting and dancing merrily around their feet. Martin raised his stick to the man and woman wrapped up in matching bright blue kagools and called a cheerful greeting.

"So you specialize in corporate law?" asked Gallagher after fussing over the dog and after the couple had moved on. "Never been interested in any other areas? You know, litigation or company law?"

"I still am, and when you're a trainee you rotate through most departments, so get to practice litigation, property, capital markets, and banking law, although naturally you're very closely monitored and managed. But in most big firms, when a trainee qualifies it's a case of putting them where the work is, not necessarily in an area the person would ideally like to practice. That's really how I ended up doing corporate law."

"You don't enjoy it?"

"I love it. But like any business, how busy we are depends on how buoyant the economy is, local and global, and when it's thriving we're flat-out with all kinds of work: mergers, joint ventures, privatizations, or companies floating on various stock exchanges. But when it's nose-diving, like it has been these past few years, we become an overhead, sitting there twiddling our thumbs. Honestly, Gallagher, being let go was like opening a window for a trapped bird."

"Would you ever consider working as legal counsel? For a company?"

"After I qualified, I only had sights set on partnership. But you soon begin to realize the chances of becoming a partner are pretty slim even for the cream of the crop. And those lucky few that make the grade pretty much give up having any kind of social life outside of work. Even then some remain purists, prefer to stay in private practice rather than escape to the corporate world. Much has to do with the fact that they'd no longer be earning fees, income for the business, and believe they'd be less valued. As a support function, you see, they essentially become an overhead. But those I've spoken to who have made the jump love it. So the answer is yes, I would consider working in-house."

Thirty minutes into the hike they passed beneath Hawk's Tor, a table of rough granite slabs set on the top of a hill of rough grass. At the apex, Anton could make out a molded stone structure, an ordnance survey trig point. He relished the idea of scrambling to the summit, but when he looked over at Martin and Gallagher, the former gently shook his head. They were still keeping close tabs on their patient. When they reached a sloping path flowing down as far as they could see, the men maintained their pace. Anton would have preferred some exertion, to pick up the pace, having missed his usual morning run. But conscious of his condition, they continued at a normal walking pace, and while Gallagher led the way out in front, Anton engaged Martin in conversation.

"How long have you two been together?" he asked.

"Twenty-one years, can you believe?" said Martin. "We met at university. I was twenty-four, Gallagher twenty-two. Federico wonders how we can stand it."

"What do you mean?" asked Anton.

"Being with the same person, day in, day out. Night after night," said Martin. "He thinks same-sex marriages are doomed to failure. Because it's the same sex with the same person."

Anton said nothing. Even though he understood himself well enough to know the arrangement would never work for him, he had met gay couples—and straight ones, come to that—who were by choice far from monogamous. Some even claimed the agreement had saved their relationships. Anton understood his heart well enough to recognize his inability to separate the physical bond from the emotional one, the sex from the love, just as he could never betray the honor and trust of a friendship. Those two aspects of a partnership had to come hand in hand. Christian and he had enjoyed a good exclusive partnering, and apart from the sex, which was mind-blowing when Christian was in the right mood, he missed the conversation and companionship.

"What Rico doesn't realize yet," continued Martin, "is that being together is not all about sex. Quite often it's as much about the companionship and the shared silences."

"He's young still," said Anton, staring off into the distance. "At some point most of us need to find some kind of permanence. I consider you two an inspiration."

"Well said," called Gallagher.

"Listen to you," said Martin with a quizzical but endearing smile. "Old soul. I bet Rico's not much younger than you."

Anton smiled to himself. An "old soul," he pondered, Martin's comment matching his grandmother's assessment of him. At the time he thought she had meant his contentment at being around people of all ages. Perhaps that formed a part of the condition. He certainly enjoyed the easy company of these two older men.

After following a number of serpentine paths, some barely discernible, the larger dirt track they had been following eventually led toward a tall but scrubby wall of hedgerows. As they neared, Anton could make out a road on the other side and spotted a small turnstile. Gallagher had clearly been leading them toward the wooden gate and waved his stick in that direction.

"Almost there," he called. "How are you feeling, Anton?"

"On top of the world," he called back and realized he did feel good, wide awake and alert, better than he had felt all week.

After climbing the turnstile, they stepped out onto a sloping road, and after following the right-hand curve for a hundred yards, the Hawk's Tavern appeared, as welcoming as an old friend. Built from a mix of local granite and stone, the long building appeared to sink into the ground at the near end in order to compensate for the gradient of the road, almost causing the sill of the closest downstairs sash window to rest on the road's surface. On the near side of the entrance, white-marked parking spaces stood empty, but the far side already housed six cars. Fixed to the wall by the entrance, a handwritten blackboard advertised the pub's daily bill of fare, and already heads and backs of regulars could be seen through the tavern's windows.

"How do they manage to get any business so far from anywhere?" asked Anton.

"Tourist trade during high season," said Martin. "And locals during the low. There's a big caravan park about a mile from here, just outside Mandeleigh village. Summer trade is fairly brisk."

As they cleaned off their boots at the front porch entrance, Anton spotted a performance car in the parking lot reserved for the pub owner, a car with a familiar number plate. He pointed out the silver Porsche to the men.

"That's the reason I ended up knocking on Stephen's door," he said. "So much for a shortcut. I might have ended up here."

"I could imagine worse places," said Gallagher.

They settled at a table near to the inglenook fireplace, a blaze of pungent logs and pinecones already well under way. Anton welcomed the homey warmth after the chill air of the moors. While Martin and Gallagher removed their jackets, Anton insisted on buying them drinks and ordering lunch. The barmaid, a stout, red-cheeked woman in her fifties, smiled warmly as she approached him. He ordered drinks, then leaned on the bar, watching her pull the first pint. Beyond her, in the corridor leading to the toilets, he spotted a wall-mounted pay phone.

"Who owns the silver Porsche out front?" asked Anton.

"That'll be the son-in-law, Mel's," she said with good humor, looking up and rolling her eyes. "Honestly, he spends more time cleaning the thing than driving it. Boys and their toys."

"Nice machine, though," said Anton.

"If you like that kind of a thrill," she remarked, peering at him, an eyebrow raised. "But try getting a weekly shop in the backseat."

After he had finished ordering food and paying, he carried the drinks to the table and then excused himself to use the pay phone.

After two rings, a male voice answered.

"Hello?" came Ewan's brusque voice.

"Ewan. It's Anton. Can I speak to Gemma?" said Anton.

No response except for a loud clunk as Ewan threw the receiver down on a hard surface. Dull, distant shouts echoed down the line.

"I tried calling you at home," said Gemma, breathless, before he had a chance to speak. He hadn't even realized she had picked up the phone. "You left your mobile here. I was cleaning out the room when they rang."

"Who?"

"The agent from Sherman and something. You were right. You've got an interview this Wednesday. They're going to e-mail you the details. Where were you?"

Anton went through the story, softening details of the accident and avoiding any mention of his blackout in Stephen's kitchen. Eventually she agreed to send the mobile to him using a courier service.

"See you at Christmas," she said, just before they said their good-byes.

As he approached the table, Martin sat alone and peered up at him.

"Trouble?" he asked, concern in his eyes. Anton had been lost in thought but realized he must have been frowning on his return from the call.

"Not really," he said, squeezing out a smirk and then shrugging for effect. "Family stuff."

Martin let out a rumble of sympathy as Anton sat down and took his first sup of the half pint of room-temperature beer. Normally, when out with friends, he would nurse a single bottle of trendy lager or splash out on a vodka lime. But the surroundings lent themselves to the rustic ale, and he soon found the taste growing on him.

"Where's Gallagher?" he asked, breaking the pause.

"He made the mistake of checking his mobile for messages," said Martin. "He's outside now, making an urgent call to his office. Honestly, one day and they can't do without him. I'm glad I'm out of all that corporate slavery. Hopefully Gal will see the light one day. Problem is he loves the work and the challenge. And he's darn good at it too."

While they waited for the food to arrive, Martin continued talking about their business together, how the first shop had been left to him by an uncle who had never married, and how between him and Gallagher they had turned the business around to make fairly healthy profits. They had two shops now and employed managers in both, which freed up Martin's time to oversee the operation and locate valuable pieces at auction or home clearances and provided ample opportunities to visit Stephen for long weekends. While Martin talked, Gallagher rejoined them at the table and chipped in about his work as head of acquisitions for the petroleum company and how he spent his evenings and a lot of weekends helping out in the shops. When he spoke about his work, his enthusiasm about the role shone through, but he was equally motivated by his association with the antique business. The man had the best of both worlds.

"So what do you make of Stephen?" asked Martin, changing tack in the brief pause.

Anton had been half expecting the question at some point or another. He had concocted a suitably noncommittal but gracious response.

"He's been very accommodating and professional," said Anton, nodding his head with sufficient seriousness.

"Come on, old man. What do you really think?" said Martin, a grin forming on his face as Gallagher laughed. "We're not radio Rico. Nothing gets repeated outside of these four walls."

Twenty-four hours ago he had known neither of these men. Already they felt like old friends who could see through his façade like a mannequin in a shop window. He had wanted to say he didn't understand Stephen, who one minute seemed fine with his uninvited guest, the next made him feel as unwelcome as an intruder.

"Honestly? I find him a little intimidating," said Anton with a sigh. What he didn't mention was that he also found the man unsettlingly attractive.

"He can be," said Martin, nodding in agreement. "We've known him a long time, so we're used to his frostiness. But as far as I'm concerned, he's allowed a certain amount of latitude after all he's been through. He's also generous enough to entertain us all out here every so often. And not only is he an incredible cook, but he also insists on chauffeuring us all around to save us the worry of driving. He's what I'd call the perfect host."

"You've obviously been friends a long time," said Anton. "He trusts you. Even I can see that. It's really nice."

"Stephen thrives on familiarity," said Martin. "It takes him forever to forge lasting friendships, but once he does he is fiercely loyal and would do anything for you. But as you witnessed, he's not easy company. Frankly, I'm surprised Sean still comes to the gatherings.

In the past the house used to be full, ten or more of us crammed in there, sleeping on sofas or floors. But over time old friends have either drifted away or cried off one too many times. And unfortunately these days Stephen prefers us not to bring new friends. Sean thinks he's a sociopath, but I think he's being a little unkind."

"Strange, though, I get the impression he likes you," said Gallagher, a casual remark that received a sharp shake of the head from Martin and sent anxious ripples through Anton.

"If so, he has an odd way of showing it. So what's the story with Sean and Federico?" asked Anton, quickly moving the subject along.

Martin glanced across the table at Gallagher.

"One for you, Gal," he said.

"Oh, Lord. Sean works at the local sports center in Oxford with my sister," said Gallagher. "They get on really well. So between the two of us we managed to coerce him into coming along to a dinner in our favorite restaurant last February, the same weekend Stephen came to visit."

"You set him up with Stephen?" said Anton, laughing in disbelief.

"He's a catch," said Gallagher with a shrug. "And he was single."

"So what happened?" asked Anton.

"What do you think? Disastrous," said Gallagher. "As I'm sure you can already tell, Sean has his own particular tastes. Worst of all, Stephen cottoned onto the ploy and, in front of everyone around the table, announced what he suspected. Of course we had to come clean. Sean took the whole thing in good spirits. Federico was waiting our table that night, so the exercise was not a complete disaster. But we had a clear warning shot from the doctor, no more meddling behind his back with blind dates."

Anton laughed along with them as the barmaid arrived carrying their meals, a shepherd's pie for Martin and Gallagher, and a ploughman's lunch for Anton. He could imagine Stephen's face at the Oxford restaurant, berating the two of them despite their well-meaning and good-hearted attempt at finding him a partner.

As his meal was placed in front of him, Anton marveled at how a simple ploughman's lunch had transformed over the years from a block of cheddar cheese, salad, pickles, a pickled onion, and half a loaf of bread to something reminiscent of a cheese board at the end of an expensive meal. Although the wooden cutting board contained pickles, salad, and a thin slice of good old English cheddar, on this modern equivalent, Brie, Roquefort, Beaufort, and Camembert overshadowed the traditionally English dairy, accompanied by a mini baguette, spicy coleslaw, shaved ham, black olives, two halves of a boiled egg, and an overgenerous wedge of gala pie. Not that he could fault the fare, which came as a welcome sight after their hike, and which they ate in satisfied silence.

"Does Stephen have a partner now?" asked Anton after taking a deep draft of beer and replacing his glass on the table.

Martin and Gallagher shared a cautious glance. He could imagine what they were thinking, about how much they should tell him, this transient who had dropped into their lives and would as quickly drop out. And moreover, was it right to talk about anything that concerned Stephen's private life without his knowledge? During the pause, Anton almost told them to forget the question, but before he could respond, Martin answered.

"He did. Sebastian. Stephen was a different person when they were together," he said. "Sebastian pulled Stephen out of a dark place. Both independent souls, but they made each other happy. Sebastian was adventurous almost to the point of addiction, always seeking out something new and challenging. Extreme sports gave him a high. If he had a mountain to paraglide off or monstrous waves to surf, he was at his happiest. Stephen would always be there, supporting and watching out for him, but you could tell he wasn't happy. Stephen hates being powerless. Sebastian tried to involve him, but Stephen knew all about the inherent risks. A part of his training, I suppose."

Anton nodded. He understood Stephen's apprehension. Christian had been the same, pushing him to do things outside his comfort zone, leaving him feeling spineless whenever he refused to join in. Sebastian must have been his equivalent of Christian, the one who turned Stephen into damaged goods.

"And is that why Sebastian left him?" asked Anton after a moment.

"Sebastian died," said Martin.

"Shit," he said, mortified, dropping his gaze to the table. "I'm sorry."

"Don't worry. You weren't to know," said Gallagher. "But it's best not to mention Sebastian's name in Stephen's presence, unless you want to risk an even worse mood."

"Last night's CD jazz collection. That belonged to Sebastian. Which is why everyone fell silent."

Neither man needed to answer because Martin's deep breath and Gallagher's wistful nod said everything. Martin eventually broke the silence with an admission.

"Doesn't help that you look a little like Sebastian. So best not to mention his name."

"Point taken. And thanks for the advice," said Anton. "I'll keep that in mind."

Not that he had any reason to bring the subject up with Stephen, but he certainly had a lot more questions he wanted to ask. Across the table from him, the men had begun to ready themselves for the return hike, so he deferred to silence.

CHAPTER 5
SPECTER

MIDAFTERNOON, ANTON climbed with newfound energy to the top of a small knoll and finally glimpsed the coach house. The racing-green Range Rover had once again appeared and stood pride of place outside. Throughout the day, Anton had felt increasingly stronger and more complete again. Scanning the cottage now, he felt a momentary twinge of anxiousness. In an effort to staunch the feeling, he pulled his digital camera from his backpack and snapped a couple of shots of the panorama. While the other men clambered up to join him, he observed the surrounding sky begin to mottle with clouds of dusty gray.

Stephen met them at the open front door as they clustered around, scraping clumps of mud off their boots. Now in formal wear of a pale blue shirt, beige chinos, and brown shoes, he looked entirely different from the man Anton had met the night before—relaxed but dapper and controlled, leaning against the doorframe, one long leg crossed over the other at the ankle. In one hand he held a floral mug. The other he used to massage the same spot at the back of his neck. Anton kept to one side, occasionally casting a nervous glance at him, waiting to follow the lead of the two older men, who took turns to use an old cast-iron boot scraper fixed into the stone paving to the right of the door. From time to time he noticed Stephen gazing at him, but on the occasions their eyes met, Anton wrenched his gaze away, pretending to inspect something on his clothing or on his boots. In the front garden, Martin grabbed a hose attached to a tap in the wall and began sloshing water over his hiking boots. As soon as Gallagher joined him, Anton stepped behind them and took his turn at the boot scraper.

"Where did you get those?" Stephen asked, frowning down at the green Wellingtons he had borrowed.

"My fault, Stephen. Hope you don't mind," called Martin, peering up from the task of untying his hiking boots. "I found them in your shoe cupboard. He only had trainers, which would have been a disaster out on the moor."

"And they fit perfectly. Once I rinse them they'll be as good as new," added Anton, grinning sheepishly at Stephen.

Stephen snorted softly, shook his head, and said, "Don't worry. I've been trying to get around to taking them and some other stuff to the charity store. Glad to see they've been put to good use."

"And as you can probably tell," said Gallagher, walking over and wrapping his arm around Anton's shoulders. "Your patient is perfectly fit and well. Managed a hike all the way to the Hawk and back."

"Punctuated by a hearty pub lunch," added Martin, joining him. "And a restorative half pint of Stubbing's Old Ale."

Stephen nodded his approval and stepped out into the garden to allow Martin and Gallagher into the house. Anton finished hosing the boots and stepped out of them onto the dry doormat, then arranged them next to Martin's. All the time, Stephen's steely blue eyes scrutinized him.

"Anton," said Martin, appearing at the front door and tapping his watch. "If you're going to book that hire car, you'd better get a move on before they close for the day."

Anton, in the process of unzipping his jacket, checked his own watch and noticed the hour: three forty-five. The day had flown by. He hesitated a moment before responding, but before he could say anything, Stephen spoke.

"Are you okay to drive?" he asked, a crinkle of concern between his eyebrows. "It's not something I would advise, even though your concussion was mild. And, more importantly, do you feel confident enough to get behind the wheel again?"

Although Anton felt perfectly well and healthy, he hadn't consciously thought about getting into a car again, let alone driving. Now that he did, a tremor of doubt snaked through him. The frown of hesitation must have shown on his face.

"Look, I'm at a conference in Southampton tomorrow," said Stephen. "If you wanted to stay another night—which I'm perfectly fine with—I can drop you off at the mainline station. I'm doing the same for Martin and Gallagher."

"That's right," said Gallagher. "The Southampton to Waterloo stops at East Croydon. You said you live in Croydon, correct?"

His mind started to reel. He had enjoyed the company of the men and appreciated their concern and generosity. But he felt like an interloper, and moreover still felt awkward around Stephen.

"That's really kind of you…," he began.

"But?" said Stephen.

"I think I'll be okay. And I don't want to overstay my welcome," he said and meant it.

"Are you absolutely sure?"

"I am. But thank you for your concern."

"Of course. Perfectly fine," said Stephen, unfolding his arms and crouching to place his mug to the side of the doorstep. Anton thought he saw something like relief in the man's face. "Martin, can you give him a hand to make the call while I clean up out here?"

Stephen stepped past the men, turned on the hose, and using a stiff garden brush and the stream of water, began to tidy up the front garden after them.

"Come on," said Martin, leading the way into the house, both of them dropping their jackets by the front door.

"I didn't offend him, did I?" asked Anton as Martin pulled the card from the hall table. "I'm never quite sure. I do have an interview to prepare for, and I thought you'd all like some time together—"

"Don't worry, old man," said Martin, squeezing his upper arm. "He's just playing the part of the concerned doctor. Here, let me dial for you."

Anton lifted the handset, grateful to Martin for dialing the number on the old-fashioned rotary dial. However, as he placed the heavy receiver to his ear, he heard no dial tone. After pushing the cradle hook a couple of times, he still had no connection.

Seeing his confusion, Martin took the handset from him, listened, and then tried again.

"Nope. Dead as a doornail," said Martin before calling out, "Stephen, did you know if your phone line's down?"

After a few seconds, Stephen hurried into the house and, without registering Anton, went through the same routine as Martin. He checked both the wires and phone but could find no fault.

"Do you have a signal on your mobile, Gallagher?" said Martin to the man lounging against the doorframe.

Stephen knelt to examine the wall socket on the skirting board.

"Not a chance in hell," said Gallagher, checking anyway. "Why do you think I like coming here so much?"

"Don't worry," said Stephen, grabbing his car keys and heading out. "Hop in the car and I'll drive you to the village. Five minutes away. They have a public phone box. You can dial from there."

Anton was caught off guard and rushed to squeeze his feet into the trainers he had left inside the door. When he reached the car, he noticed Stephen glaring angrily out of the front windscreen. As he opened the door and dropped into the passenger seat, Stephen spat out a soft curse.

"This is bloody ridiculous," he said, turning the key in the silent ignition again and then thumping the steering wheel. "She ran fine this morning."

Anton was about to sympathize and offer some suggestions but, seeing Stephen's mood, decided to remain quiet. Stephen reached down beneath the dash, popped open the bonnet, and jumped out of the car. For a few minutes he busied himself toying with the engine, then walked around, jumped back in, and tried the ignition again. Still the engine did not come to life. Finally, after another series of muttered words, he strode to the rear of the vehicle, brought a toolbox back with him, and continued working beneath the bonnet of the car.

After sitting and waiting for five minutes, Anton decided to get out of the car. He considered going around the front to help Stephen but knew he would have little to offer except moral support. Eventually he joined the other men, who stood watching from the front gate.

"Somebody doesn't want you to leave," said Martin as he joined them.

While they stood there, a distant crack of thunder broke the quietness, and the gathered rainclouds began to empty their payload. Within seconds, a combination of heavy rain and hail began to pummel the ground.

"Indoors," cried Gallagher, the first to turn and head for the dry sanctuary of the cottage. Anton hesitated for an imprudently long moment, while Martin had already followed on the heels of his partner.

"Someone get me an umbrella," shouted Stephen to nobody in particular.

Being the nearest, Anton decided to oblige. Already standing in the doorway, Martin yanked a huge yellow golf umbrella from the stand, which he handed to Anton. By the time he had struggled to get the thing open and reached Stephen, both of them were drenched. Standing helpless next to the busy doctor, Anton checked his watch again and felt oddly relieved, as if someone had made his mind up for him.

"Stephen," he said through the hiss and clatter of rain on the car body and gravel road. "It's too late now anyway. If it's okay with you, I'll take you up on your offer and stay another night. Head back by train tomorrow."

Stephen's voice growled from beneath the bonnet. "Unless I get this bloody thing running, nobody's going anywhere today or tomorrow. Try the ignition again, will you?"

He handed the umbrella to Stephen, took the car keys, and ran around to the driver's seat. Once seated in front of the steering wheel, a sudden anxiousness filled him, something that took him by surprise. Where he used to feel usual and comfortable and in control, he experienced indecision and a tremor of dread. Perhaps he wasn't ready to drive just yet. After slotting the key into the switch with a shaky hand and turning it, once again nothing happened; the engine remaining dormant. While twisting the key back, ready to try again, he peered through the windscreen in time to witness a breathtaking streak of wild lightning crackle across the skyline, illuminating the darkened sky. For some reason, his gaze spun toward the cottage, and in the split second of bright light, he thought he saw an indistinct figure in the upstairs bedroom to the far right, gazing down, a lit cigarette in one hand. But the flash of light faded as quickly as it had exploded into being, and when he blinked away the flash shadow and looked back up, apart from plain white curtains on either side, the window remained dark and empty.

He sighed deeply, closed his eyes, and leaned forward to rest his forehead on the arc of the steering wheel before deciding to try the ignition one last time. On this occasion two things happened simultaneously. The Range Rover's engine roared to life, and the telephone in the house began to ring.

The slam of the bonnet startled Anton, bringing him upright and tumbling back in the driver's seat. Within seconds Stephen appeared, breathless, at the open car window.

"Sorry about this. I can still get you to a mainline station," he said, his damp blond hair hanging into his eyes. "I'm sure there's a late train—"

"Honestly, if it's all the same with you," said Anton, turning the engine off. "I'd really rather stay."

"Good," said Stephen, a broad smile lighting up his rain-speckled face. "And now we have a working phone and car, not only can I book an extra place at Arianne's—the best French restaurant for miles, by the way—but I can also drive us there."

"On one condition," said Anton, grinning back.

"Yes?" asked Stephen, a crease starting to form between his brows.

"You let me pay. For all the trouble I've caused."

"You'll have to fight Martin and Gallagher for that privilege," said Stephen, smiling again and opening the door to allow Anton to share the umbrella with him. "First of all, though, we'd both better get out of these wet clothes and into a hot shower. Climb under here with me."

Anton jumped down and shut the door, then leaned into Stephen's warm body, trying hard not to make physical contact, smelling a musky mix of damp wool and antiseptic soap and hoping the man did not notice the flush rise in his cheeks. As they reached the cottage, Martin stood in the doorframe.

"Stephen. Your mother's on the phone," he said, his voice solemn. "Doesn't sound good."

CHAPTER 6
FATHER

EVEN THOUGH damp through, Anton huddled at the kitchen table with Martin and Gallagher, waiting for Stephen to finish his call. None of them spoke, each casting cautious glances toward the door. Like accomplices, they sat listening to the indistinct murmur of Stephen's deep voice from the hallway. When he eventually appeared in the kitchen doorway, he looked pale and drawn.

"Father had a stroke," he said, his brows furrowing. "They've been trying to call me. He's in the ICU at Exeter General. Wouldn't have been my first choice, but my mother and sister were there with him at the time, and it's local. I spoke to the physician, and he says he's stable. But I need to go and check on him."

"Of course you do. And we'll all come with you," said Martin firmly and, without needing to ask, echoing the sentiment of them all. "Keep you company."

"No," said Stephen, calm but irrefutable. "I'd rather do this alone. I'll drop you off at the restaurant. It's on the way. No point in all of us missing out on dinner. Exeter's about a thirty minute drive from there, so I can join you for coffee on the way back."

Together Martin and Gallagher began to protest. At one point, as the men tried to argue a number of compromises, including finding a restaurant in Exeter after the visit, getting takeaway on the way home, or one of them stopping home and cooking, Stephen's weary gaze settled on Anton, who had sat quietly the whole time.

"What do you think, Anton?" he asked.

Anton had been considering his own mother and father, how they had died in an air crash on a trip to Ireland, and how he had never been given a chance to say good-bye. Close family support had meant everything at the time and especially during the painful months after their funerals.

"It's not really my place—"

"Perhaps not, but I'd like to hear what you think anyway."

"Then I agree with you, Stephen," he said, nodding slowly. "We'd only be in the way. At times like this you need to be with your family, to have them around you."

"Exactly."

Part of him wondered why Stephen had asked for his opinion, but the smile of gratitude he received warmed Anton, and he could not help but grin back.

"Looks like the two of you have already decided," said Martin, frowning quizzically at Anton.

"Sorry, Martin," said Anton, putting a hand on the man's shoulder, not wanting to sully their recently wrought friendship. "I know it's not really for me to say. But that's what I would want, if I were in the same position."

"It is what I want," said Stephen.

"In which case," sighed Gallagher, "I'd rather we postponed Arianne's until we return in December for Christmas. This was supposed to be your treat, Stephen, to say thanks. We'll stay here, and I can knock something together. As long as I can raid your wine cellar."

"Do you mind if I have a change of heart too?" said Anton, addressing Stephen. "As you're heading into Exeter anyway, I might as well get the late train into London. If you don't mind dropping me near the mainline station on your way."

"Are you sure?" said Martin. "Admittedly Gallagher's culinary skills are no match for Stephen's—or Arianne's, come to that—but he can cobble together a pretty decent Brie and pickle sandwich."

"Thanks for the vote of confidence," muttered Gallagher, raising his eyebrows at Martin and then winking. "But if the boy wants to go, we should let him."

"As I said earlier, you're more than welcome to stay, Anton," said Stephen, his gentle eyes studying Anton's.

"No, this makes perfect sense," replied Anton, smiling and nodding. "And more importantly, you'll have someone to keep you company on the drive there."

"That's settled, then. Don't want to hassle you, but we'll need to get going soon. Go grab a hot shower and then bring your things down," said Stephen, initially to Anton but then turning to Martin and Gallagher. "I should be back by around ten thirty. We can have a drink together, and I'll probably be ready to have a bite to eat by then."

"It's a deal," said Gallagher.

Anton showered quickly and met Martin and Gallagher by the front door. Oddly enough, he felt a pang of regret bidding them good-bye. Unwittingly, they had helped him through a difficult time with their common sense advice and selfless support.

"Now do you have everything?" asked Martin like a mother hen.

"Yes, Martin. All present and correct."

"And how are you feeling?" asked Gallagher.

"After the shower, fantastic. Like a million dollars."

"It's over an hour to the hospital. Do you need the loo before you go?"

"Martin, stop fussing," said Gallagher, chuckling along with Anton.

"I'm fine, thanks."

"Okay, young man," said Martin, reaching out, giving him a hug and a couple of slaps on the back. Once he let go, he reached into his jacket pocket for a card. "You need to promise to stay in touch. Here's our card, telephone and e-mail details. Drop us a line or give us a call to let us know you got back safely. And if you're ever in Oxford, come and visit."

"Or if you just need a break from the grind of job hunting," said Gallagher, taking his turn to hug Anton. "We'd be more than happy to have you stay with us in Oxford."

Outside in the failing light, dark rainclouds had retreated to the horizon replaced by a fairground sky full of shimmering stars, and an air of damp freshness. While Anton tossed his bags into the back of the car, Stephen climbed into the front, and he heard him take a deep breath before turning the key in the ignition. This time, fortunately, the engine roared to life, and Anton could not help but let out a gentle chuckle as he slammed the back door closed. Before getting into the car, he turned to see Gallagher and Martin standing at the front door, seeing him off. As he waved, the lights inside the entryway flickered, causing both men to turn, check, and then share a laugh together.

During the car ride, neither man spoke as the Range Rover sped through the darkened lanes in the failing light. Stephen kept his eyes fixed on the road, either concentrating on driving or lost in thought. In the warmth from the heater, Anton let himself relax and closed his eyes. He had no way of checking if a nonstop train went from Exeter to London but figured that, even if he had to make a couple of station changes, he could be home before or just after midnight.

"About another hour," said Stephen.

When he opened his eyes, the doctor was peering at him, as though reading his mind.

"Traffic willing, I should be able to get you to the station before six thirty. My sister does the London run all the time. Trains run regularly up until about eight thirty."

"Perfect," said Anton, more encouraged. "Thanks, Stephen."

Once again they continued, unspeaking. This time Anton decided to break the silence.

"How old is he? Your father?" he asked.

"Seventy-three," said Stephen. "But he's enjoyed good health his whole life. I force him to have a checkup each year. Came as quite a shock. For everyone."

"I bet," said Anton.

"A minor stroke. Ischemic, not hemorrhagic. Not as serious. Although there's always the possibility of future complications. But I'm sure he'll make a full recovery," said Stephen. The mollifying words tumbling out of him contrasted sharply with his tone, strained and barely controlled. "He's always been a tough bastard. Hard as nails. Ran a tight ship at home but was always there when I needed him. Probably just a scare. But I need to be there."

"Of course you do," said Anton, studying him. "Are you sure you're okay, Stephen?"

"Yes," he said, but he didn't sound fine. "Do you mind if we stop at the service station up ahead? I could do with five minutes."

"Thank goodness," said Anton, the dull ache in his bladder becoming more urgent with the knowledge of an impending break. "I know I went just before we left, but I need the bathroom again."

They pulled into the darkened service station car park, and as soon as Stephen had switched off the engine, Anton opened the car door. Stephen sat behind the wheel unmoving.

"You coming?" said Anton.

"No," said Stephen, frozen in place. "I'm fine. Just needed a quick breather."

When Anton returned to the car, whistling in the cold night air, he noticed Stephen's silhouette through the windscreen, his forehead resting on the steering wheel. He thought for a moment the doctor had fallen asleep. But when he opened the door, he heard him gently sobbing, a sound that wrenched Anton's heart.

"Oh, God, Stephen," he said, jumping into the seat, turning him around, and pulling Stephen's head onto his shoulder, wrapping his arm around his back. Unexpectedly, the doctor didn't resist but allowed himself to be held and put his arms around Anton's waist. They stayed that way for a while, Anton rubbing circles into Stephen's back until his sobs subsided and his breathing became more even.

"I can't lose him too, Anton," he said, pulling his head away, the words a gentle whisper.

"You won't, I'm sure," said Anton, releasing his arms, relieved to hear the man more controlled and also suddenly grateful he had insisted on accompanying him. "You said he's always been in good health. Surely that counts for something. But I'm no expert, so I'd have to check with a reputable doctor. Happen to know any?"

The remark produced the reaction he had hoped for, and after managing a soft chuckle, Stephen took a deep breath and relaxed. He faced forward again but glanced nervously at Anton a couple of times, his eyes still glazed with tears.

"Sorry," he said, wiping his eye with the knuckle of his forefinger. "Not exactly setting a great example, am I? I know I should be used to this kind of thing. I deal with much worse every day."

"This is your father, Stephen," said Anton. "It's completely natural. And anyway, where does it say in the Hippocratic oath that doctors aren't allowed to be human every once in a while?"

"Still," said Stephen, getting himself under control. "I'm sorry you had to see that."

"You have no reason to be," said Anton. "Do you want me to drive for a bit? I promise not to chase any sports cars."

"No, it's fine," said Stephen, laughing gently again and starting the engine. "I mean, I'm fine."

"Good," said Anton, taking a deep breath and making up his mind. "In which case, you'd better talk fast about your family. Your father, mother, and sister. If I'm going to meet them at the hospital."

"Sorry?" said Stephen, confused at first and then frowning. "No, Anton. You don't need to—"

"I know I don't need to, but I'm going to anyway," he said, adamant. Without a second thought, the man had taken him into his care and helped get him fixed up. Reciprocation was the least he could do.

"You'll miss the last train," said Stephen, sitting still, the engine idling.

"I know. You didn't think I was going to let you drive back alone? Not when you've got all this to deal with," said Anton. "What kind of a friend would do such a thing?"

"Anton, are you sure?" said Stephen, still not convinced but his objection softening.

"Drive," said Anton in a mock serious tone. "Otherwise visiting hours will be over. And this whole road trip will have been in vain."

At this last remark, Stephen snorted softly and shook his head but then put the car in gear and headed out into the stream of evening traffic. During the journey Stephen gave Anton the lowdown on his family while warning Anton that he would probably not be allowed into the ward. More importantly for Anton, the simple act of getting Stephen to talk about his family seemed to lift his spirits, telling tales of one familial adventure or another, causing Anton to laugh aloud, which put them both in a good mood. By the time they pulled into the hospital car park at around six thirty, Anton had warmed to a family most of whom he had never met.

As expected, the receptionist confirmed that only close family members could visit Mr. Miller senior, and in truth, Anton was quietly relieved. He could not imagine Stephen's father being happy about having a complete stranger seeing him wired up to machines. Before Stephen left, Anton grabbed his elbow and insisted he stay until visiting hours had ended and not worry about him. Grabbing a magazine from the wall rack instead, he settled himself on one of the vacant easy chairs in the half-full waiting room and flicked through it absently. Hospital odors of pungent disinfectants, bleached floors, and medical gauze seemed to overpower other unrecognizable smells, and he wondered for a moment if Stephen relished the association with these everyday scents—or even noticed them at all. In Anton's youth, not long after his parents had died, his grandmother had bought him a set of oil paints, and the smell had initially made him gag. But after completing a couple of paintings from photographs he had taken or from memory and discovering a talent within himself, albeit minor, he had begun to associate the smell with creativity and self-expression.

After half an hour, while putting the magazine back, he decided he needed a coffee from the vending machine. He fished in his pocket for coins, and as he brought out a handful, he sensed someone standing next to him. Stepping to one side, he turned to see a pretty young blonde woman standing there, observing him.

"Sorry," he said, pulling a face. "Sometimes feel I need a course on how to operate these things. All for a cup of coffee. Do you want to go first?"

"You're Anton," she said, grinning.

He stared, confused, wondering if he ought to know her from somewhere.

"Yes. Sorry," he said. "Have we met?"

"No," she said, holding out her hand. "I'm Susanna, Stephen's sister. He asked me to come and keep an eye on you. Make sure you didn't get up to any mischief. Looks like I failed."

Of course, thought Anton. The resemblance was plain: the same strong features, beautiful eyes, and almost bleached-blond hair. Except where Stephen's attraction was strongly chiseled and masculine, Susanna had an elegance, her face intelligent and capable but her whole being quintessentially feminine.

"Did he now?" said Anton, warming to her. "In which case, can I get you a coffee? As long as you can help me work this thing."

After a couple of aborted attempts, during which a small queue had built up behind them, they took their cappuccinos to a couple of spare seats and chatted like old friends.

"Surprised I've never heard of you before," said Susanna, wrapping her elegant fingers around the Styrofoam cup. "Stephen's usually quite vocal about his friends."

"Let's just say I'm an honorary member of the group," said Anton.

"I see. So he's making new friends again?" said Susanna, impressed. "That's progress. Since Sebastian passed away and that whole dreadful business afterwards, he hasn't bothered getting out much."

"So Martin said," he replied, wondering fleetingly what the "whole dreadful business" she referred to could mean. "But I kind of stumbled into their lives. By accident, not by choice. Literally."

He went on to retell the story about the accident and the men's generous help. In addition, he mentioned his original plan to get the late train back into London and last minute change of heart, although he didn't elaborate on the reason.

"Good decision. You wouldn't have made the late train," she said. "We live in Beaconsfield, my husband Bob and our three little gremlins. We only have the one car, so whenever I visit Mum and Dad without Bob, I take the train down. And the last one leaves just after eight. Luckily we're all down for the week, for a break. Bob's looking after the kids tonight, so I have the car."

"Bit of a bombshell for you all," said Anton. "Stephen took the news badly."

"Did he?" she said, gazing away, lost in thought. "Yes, I suppose he would have. I wonder if he might have a change of heart about next year. I know he's committed, but I'm sure they'd make concessions under exceptional circumstances. It is voluntary work, after all."

"What's happening next year?" asked Anton.

"He didn't tell you?" she asked, taken slightly aback, but then her face softened. "I suppose not. He's taking a year off to work in Africa for an international charity. Something he'd planned to do ever since Sebastian died. And God knows, he needs a fresh start. That's why he's been winding down his practice in Southampton."

"What about the cottage?" asked Anton, trying to mask his disappointment.

"Not sure, but I think he plans to sell," she said. "Shame really, after all the work they put into the place."

Anton nodded his agreement but said nothing. They continued chatting, Anton asking her about some of the stories Stephen had told him about their family to lighten the mood and getting in return an embellished version that had them both laughing.

Later on, when Stephen appeared, he spotted them straightaway. Anton found himself grinning back when Stephen caught his eye and winked. Susanna didn't miss the gesture either. On his way to them, he stopped for a brief but cordial talk with one of the nurses. Watching him across the room, chatting and laughing affably with a completely captivated professional, Anton warmed to the man in a whole new way. Once he had joined them, conversation inevitably turned to Stephen's father.

"No paralysis, thankfully. Already arguing with Mum about letting him go home. They'll keep him under observation for a couple of nights, but he'll probably be home before the weekend. She's going to stay on for another hour. Can I leave you with them, Susie? I've got Martin and Gallagher waiting back at home."

"Of course. We're all staying down until Friday," she replied. "But you'll have to be on call next week, doctor duck. Bob has to work."

After saying their good-byes, Susanna kept Stephen back in the entranceway to the hospital for a few private parting words, while Anton waited for him outside in the cold night. Fresh air provided an instant relief from the cloying odors of the hospital waiting room. From time to time, he turned to watch them, seeing Susanna chatting animatedly with her brother. At one point she tugged Stephen's sleeve and nodded out through the glass doors, toward Anton. When he saw Stephen turn and both of them smiling at him, he wondered what had been said and could not help but grin shyly back.

Back in the car, as Anton closed the door and clipped on his seat belt, Stephen sat behind the steering wheel unmoving, staring out at the clear night sky. After a lengthy pause, Anton began to feel anxious.

"Are you all right, Stephen?" he asked, turning to him.

"Yes," Stephen replied calmly and quietly, before turning to face Anton and grinning. "Apparently I am. Thank you again, Anton."

"Come on. After all you've done for me," said Anton. Their faces were so close, both staring into the other's eyes, that Anton would have only had to lean in a fraction to kiss the doctor's beautiful mouth. Instead, vaguely embarrassed at his own thoughts, he dropped eye contact and breathed out a chuckle. "But we'd better hurry back before Gallagher burns the cheese on toast."

Stephen let his gaze hover a moment longer before turning away and starting the engine.

On the journey back, Stephen became far more relaxed and asked Anton questions about his own family. Unlike the Millers, the history of the Swann family contained tragedies: his parents' untimely death, the recent loss of his grandmother, who had pretty much brought them up single-handedly, his sister's divorce and subsequent remarriage. Anton preferred not to talk too much about himself, because everything he could think of sounded uninteresting or maudlin. Even so, he had plenty of other stories to tell that managed to fill the journey.

They entered the lane heading toward the coach house via a different route, and Anton was surprised at how quickly the time had passed. Tonight another car appeared on the road speeding toward them, and only as the vehicle drew level could they identify it as a police car. The driver slowed briefly, and both officers inside scanned them and nodded before speeding off into the night.

"Good to see the police patrolling the countryside," said Anton.

"They rarely do," said Stephen, his brow crinkling. "At least, not for as long as I can remember."

When they arrived back, the hall light still burned inside the house, and while Stephen parked, Martin opened the front door. Anton wondered for a moment how he would explain his return. As soon as the car came to a halt, he jumped out and pushed open the garden gate.

"Surprise," he said, holding his arms out and sensing Stephen entering behind.

"Hardly," said Martin, laughing and holding up Anton's small backpack. "You weren't going to get very far without this. Your wallet and front door keys are inside. You left it in the upstairs bathroom, silly boy. I spied it while Gallagher was cooking dinner. Doing a spot of spring cleaning to stay out of the chef's hair. Too late to do anything about it by then."

Anton stared at the item, his mouth drawn down in confusion. He was certain he had placed the backpack in the car, along with his overnight bag and suit. Certainly he had brought everything downstairs before leaving, and unlike his sister, he was rarely forgetful. Was this a symptom of his concussion? Yes, he had showered before leaving but felt sure he hadn't brought the backpack into the bathroom with him. Why would he need to? While Martin turned and reentered the house, Stephen placed a warm hand on his shoulder and echoed Anton's thoughts.

"Strange," said the doctor. "I could have sworn I saw you put that in the back of the car."

"Thank you," said Anton, exhaling a breath and turning to him. "I thought I was going crazy for a moment there. Thank goodness it's not just me who's hallucinating."

While following the men toward the kitchen, Martin pulled Stephen back into the hallway for a quiet word. Inside the kitchen, the table held a bottle of red uncorked, and Gallagher was in the process of placing two covered plates of food onto place mats. When Anton entered he raised his head and smiled playfully.

"Seems like you can't stay away, young man," he said. "And I'm guessing it's because you were tempted by the promise of my culinary skills. Where's Stephen?"

"Martin's talking to him," said Anton.

"Ah," said Gallagher, studying Anton, his grin slipping, eventually shaking his head. "We had a little incident. Martin thought he heard someone or something rummaging around out back in the stables. Thought it best to call the police."

"The patrol car? We saw it on the road," said Anton. From the hallway, he heard Stephen's voice raised in anger.

"They had a good look around but didn't find anything," he replied, looking anxiously at the doorway. "Probably the resident ghost finally making a guest appearance."

Just then Stephen strode into the kitchen, his face pale, his features dark and menacing. Anton had not seen this side of him and decided he never wanted to be on the receiving end. Purposefully, the doctor strode to the back of the kitchen, yanked open a drawer, and pulled out a large stainless steel torch from a drawer. He then fished keys from his pocket and unlocked a cabinet near the back door. From inside he pulled out a shotgun. Standing near the doorway,

Martin shook his head at Gallagher, as though he regretted having said anything.

"They did a thorough search, Stephen," pleaded Martin. "I went with them. We found nothing. I was obviously mistaken."

"For Christ's sake, Martin! You know what happened before. If those blood-sucking hacks are going to start up all that bloody nonsense again, I am not going to sit by and do nothing. Not this time," said Stephen angrily, unlocking the back door at the end of the kitchen.

"In which case, I'll come with you," said Martin and followed Stephen out into the darkness.

As the door closed behind them, Anton turned to Gallagher, a shock of questions on his face.

"Long story. Let's just say that a couple of years ago he had a problem with professional prowlers," he said. "Nothing stolen, nothing broken into, nobody hurt. That was never the intent. More to do with invasion of privacy. And a nasty experience like that is not one you easily forget."

"He has a shotgun?" asked Anton, horrified.

"Don't worry," said Gallagher with a smirk. "More for show than anything. It's not even loaded. He uses it to scare."

"His expression was enough for me. Heaven help the poor soul that comes up against that. If it was me, I'd run a mile and then some," said Anton, sitting at the table and causing Gallagher to chuckle again.

When the men returned ten minutes later, having found nothing, everyone sat down to eat in careful silence, Stephen providing the succinct but uninspired highlights of his visit to the hospital. However, for the rest of the meal he kept his gaze focused on his plate, his brows knotted and shoulders hunched. The other men engaged Anton in trivial conversation, goading him about his forgetfulness. Neither of them managed to lighten the mood, even after a meal of salmon en croute and a couple of glasses of particularly good Spanish red.

That night Anton slept fitfully, waking to each creak and groan of the old house. At around two thirty, he wandered out to use the bathroom, but before turning right this time, peered to the far end of the corridor. This night no light shone from beneath Stephen's door.

In the morning, after breakfast, while Martin washed up and Stephen made another check of the back of his property, Gallagher and Anton loaded their belongings into the car. Before closing the back, Anton made a purposeful check of his bags in front of the man, counting out each of them to a playfully grinning Gallagher. Although the bad mood of the previous night had lifted, they traveled to Southampton mainline station largely unspeaking, a radio news channel filling the silence.

"Thanks for everything, Stephen. Or should that be doctor duck?" said Anton with a quizzical grin, standing in the chill air on the pavement outside the train station ticket hall.

Stephen's gaze of brooding concentration softened into a smile. Moments before, Anton thought the doctor would remain in the car, because as soon as they parked he had made his farewells to them all, remaining behind the wheel as he took a call on his mobile. At the last minute, however, he jumped out and joined them.

"One of Susie's kid's pet name for me. From a children's book, apparently," he replied, shaking his head. "Not terribly respectful, is it?"

"Oh, I don't know. Could be worse," said Anton. "My niece calls me Prince Naveen. I had no idea why until one night babysitting, when she insisted on watching a Disney film. *The Princess and the Frog*. Turns out the character Prince Naveen is a good-looking but smarmy, arrogant, lazy schmuck. Kids can be cruel."

Stephen laughed aloud but quickly became serious again.

"Look, Anton," he said, his stormy blue eyes studying him. "I didn't get a proper chance to thank you… shit!"

Before he could continue, his phone rang again. He glanced at the display and then indicated with a grimace and tilt of his head that he needed to take the call. While he turned his back to Anton and stepped away, Martin poked his head out of the booking office doorway.

"The London Waterloo leaves in fifteen minutes," he called, waving Anton over. "Platform two. If you rush, you'll be able to make it. Gallagher's saving a place in the queue."

Five minutes later, ticket in hand, Anton stepped out into the daylight to bid Stephen farewell.

Both he and the Rover had already gone.

CHAPTER 7
HOME

ARRIVING OUTSIDE his apartment block early Tuesday afternoon, Anton scooped up his holdall from the backseat of the cab and paid the driver. On his train journey into Croydon, the weather had improved progressively, overcast still but free from rain. Normally he would have been pleased to get back to his small but comfortable apartment, his own private refuge bought with the money Christian had raised to buy him out of their three-bedroom house in Wandsworth. But one thought kept niggling him, that he should have shown Stephen more respect and gratitude, should have at least made the effort to stay in touch. Had she been alive, his grandmother would have scolded him for such a blatant lack of manners. But the doctor had driven off before he'd had the chance, and his disappointment had ridden with him all the way home.

In the entrance to the block, he opened his mailbox and pulled out a handful of post, sorting out the garishly colored fliers from bills and other post. One large square envelope caught his eye, his name handwritten in beautiful penmanship. After tossing the circulars into a conveniently situated bin, he tore open the flap and pulled out an invitation.

His ex-colleague, Sally Wallon, had invited him to the opening of her husband's new gallery, Brandon Wallon Art Warehouse, on New King's Road on Saturday afternoon, showcasing his work and that of his contemporaries. Champagne and canapés would be served. Sally never allowed an event to go by without the accompaniment of bubbles. She had penned in the bottom right corner, "No need to RSVP. You're coming!"

At first he smiled, knowing Sally's welcome and warmth would cheer him, that she would take him in hand and provide a detailed, exclusive, and dramatically overembellished rundown of gossip from his old firm. But then, of course, he had the sudden realization that he would be going alone. Over the past eighteen months he had declined or ignored any invitations to large gatherings, partly because those from mutual friends entailed the possibility of running into Christian and his new partner, but mostly because he hated the self-consciousness and desperation of being almost thirty and still single.

While sorting through other letters, he climbed the two flights of stairs up to his apartment. Inside, things remained exactly as he had left them: his two pairs of cross trainers stationed by the front door, his silver laptop sitting open on the coffee table, russet cushions piled up on one end of the black leather sofa where he could comfortably watch the television, and a tied-up bundle of magazines on the small dining table that he had meant to put in the recycle bin.

He dropped his bag on the floor and tossed the bills onto the table, but then went to the small kitchen and pinned the invitation prominently on the cork notice board.

With a deep sigh, he thought back over the weekend. If the accident, however minor, had taught him anything, it was that he needed to start living his life again. More importantly, Sally, who had never met Christian, remained one of the few work colleagues he made an effort to keep in touch with. She had been a nonjudgmental shoulder to cry on during his breakup and subsequent redundancy. In his diminished circle of friends, Sally was a true friend, a keeper.

On his way into the living room he noticed the crimson light of his old answering machine blinking on the hall stand. When he pressed the play button, the box announced four messages and automatically went on to play each in turn.

The polished voice of a secretary from the recruitment agency reminded him about an interview with Sharman and Walsh on Wednesday, repeating the time, address, and asking him to call to confirm. After jotting down the details on the envelope of his telephone bill, he pressed the Delete key.

A second message was from his sister. She sounded tired and had called to tell him about leaving his mobile phone behind, repeating back the call from his agent, and then, after a pause, apologizing for doubting him about his reason for leaving sooner. When he deleted the message, he felt guilt rise in his throat at her apology. At the time, she had been right.

The third message was the quietly concerned voice of Julie, Paul's girlfriend, sounding as though she was calling from inside the Standard on Sunday night, the clink of glasses and genial clamor her soundtrack. She explained how they'd tried his mobile phone but nobody had answered. Shaking his head at his thoughtlessness, he decided he would call her as soon as he'd listened to all the voice messages.

The last one burst loud and offensive from someone unknown. Clearly the man had begun speaking before the answering machine tone sounded. The voice came across harsh, garbled, and drunk.

"...like a fucking fool, do you? Do you? Better watch yourself. Else I will come round if I find out he's been there. Fucking watch if I don't. I know exactly where you live—"

Without hesitation, Anton pressed the Delete key. Crazy was the last thing he needed. Part of him felt sympathy for the true intended victim of the rant. Clearing the message bank, he phoned back the recruitment agency, followed immediately by a quick chat with Julie, which included an apology and an explanation for not showing up at the pub on Sunday night. Last of all, he sent Martin and Gallagher an e-mail to thank them, to tell them he'd arrived home safely—as promised—and to ask for Stephen's contact details. Satisfied at last, he treated himself to a long, hot shower.

With much of the afternoon remaining, he decided to get some chores out of the way, loading up the washing machine, getting a haircut, food shopping, paying outstanding bills, before having a general tidy up of the apartment. Later he would also check the status of his car with the insurance company. Doubtless there would be a mound of paperwork to complete.

Wednesday's interview with Sharman and Walsh went badly. One of the partners interviewing him, a white-haired American, seemed to take an instant and personal dislike. Instead of probing his past experience, he insisted on coming back to the fact that Anton had not secured a job in six months, and would not take the response of "waiting for the right opportunity" as credible. When faced with a question about his mobility as a single man and whether he would consider the opportunity to work in their New York office, he stated his preference to remain in London. Unable to give them a convincing enough reason for this, especially as a single unencumbered male, and not wanting to tell them the truth about his fear of flying, the interest of the remaining partners waned noticeably. Eventually he resorted to short answers, polite but not exactly forthcoming. As expected, the recruitment agency called him on Friday and said the firm decided he was not the right fit. Perhaps that was true. But a fit had to work both ways, for the firm and the solicitor. And he decided they were not good enough for him either.

By Saturday, suffering two days of domestic claustrophobia, he made up his mind to venture out. He called Sally at nine thirty in the morning to ask how early he could comfortably arrive for the gallery opening. Despite her plea for him to come over right away, they agreed to meet at around five thirty, half an hour before the official opening and time enough for them to catch up.

Determined to feel good, he pulled out his newer items of clothing and tried them on, one by one, to see what might be a good combination. He ended up picking a white cotton shirt with light blue pencil lines running vertically, a thin navy silk tie, stonewashed jeans, brown brogues and matching belt, and a navy woolen jacket. In the mirror, together with his new haircut, he liked what he saw, the epitome of smart casual.

Due to his usual reliance on the convenience of a car, he messed up the public transport connections and did not arrive at the venue until the gallery had already opened. Luckily, Sally spotted him and met him at the double front doors. She looked dazzling in her white pencil dress with red polka dots and shoulder-length auburn hair and dragged him past a number of early guests to a table of drinks.

"Look at you!" he said after she had pushed a flute of champagne into his hand. "Miss Betty Boop."

"Shit, I was going for Jayne Mansfield. Anyway, you can talk!" she replied, after pecking him on the cheek and clinking glasses with him. "Unemployment clearly agrees with you."

"Only if you mean I have more time to hunt for bargains and try things on," he said. "Then yes, it agrees with me. Sorry to be late. I'm car-less right now. Thought I'd be here well before six."

"Oh crap, is that the time?" she said, checking her stylish, sparkling red wristwatch. "Come have a look at Brandon's wall, and then I've got to mingle."

Her husband worked with acrylics, producing modern abstract pieces painted onto circular canvases of varying sizes, like a sea of bubbles, except that each had a distinctly Asian feel. Incorporating other elements, such as thin strips of bamboo, dried leaves, and sand, he used only three colors in each piece: red, black, and white. Anton had never really warmed to abstract art, something all of the displayed artists except one preferred, and his attention kept turning to the far wall, where there stood a solitary column of moody seascapes, wild collaborations of grays, blacks, and blues, at the same time natural and somber.

"What do you think?" she asked, standing at his shoulder.

"I'm no art critic," said Anton, trying to be diplomatic. "But they're interesting in a sort of contemporary way, eye-catching and bold. And if I'm not mistaken, he's worked an Asian influence into all the pieces, Japanese perhaps. Is that right?"

"No idea," said Sally and then leaned in and lowered her voice. "I know I'm supposed to be supportive, but they look like psychedelic gobstoppers to me."

"Bad girl," said Anton, laughing and knocking shoulders with her. He missed her directness, her ditzy way of bringing things back down to earth.

"It stinks not having you around at work," she said, suddenly somber. "You made it bearable. Everyone's so serious now. People stay late even if they don't need to, until the partners have gone for the evening. Kind of a 'face time' thing. You're lucky to have escaped. How's the job hunt coming along?"

"About as successful as the boyfriend hunt."

"Well, something's agreeing with you, darling," she said, smiling. "You seem a lot more relaxed and cheerful than the last time we met. Your post-Christian blues."

"Was I really that bad?"

"You were in the depression phase of the breakup, Ant," she said. "No point in me doing anything but listening. Even Oprah couldn't have helped. Seems like you're in a good place right now, either the acceptance or the healing stage."

"You believe all that crap?" he asked, even though he had a sudden realization that she was right. After the events of the unplanned weekend, he felt different, more real, more substantial.

"Don't knock it. Grief is a natural process all sensitive people go through," she said before checking her watch again. "Look, hon, have a browse around for an hour while I go and hang on to Brandon's sleeve. Play the adoring wife. And then we can have a real chitchat."

After she had gone, Anton drifted around the room, stopping eventually at the seascapes. Each side of the large square column housed three paintings, and each carried a unique fascination. Interested in studying the brushstrokes as well as viewing the picture from a few paces back, Anton found himself quickly engrossed in the collection. In the corner of each, the signature of E. D. Collingwood appeared, beautifully inscribed in red paint. On one side of the column he spotted a brooding depiction of a lone surfer out on a huge wave, somewhere that looked like Porthtowan Beach in Cornwall, a place Anton knew intimately from his childhood. Although on first glance he felt the freedom and total concentration of the surfer, after stepping back he took in the whole painting. From back there, a new emotion swept through him, an overwhelming sense of loneliness and isolation, something so close to how he had been feeling of late that his throat became dry.

"Anton" came a warmly familiar voice from behind that sent his heart racing.

He turned and found Christian smiling at him.

Dressed in his trademark casuals, black jeans and tight oatmeal sweater, his shoulder-length black locks curling down to the crew neck, he shone as beautiful and unobtainable as the last day Anton had seen him. Apart from his face appearing a little drawn, he had the same half smile, charming enough to melt a room full of art critics, his eyes both mischievous and treacherous.

"How have you been?" he asked, his gaze traveling down Anton's body, making him tremble at the visceral touch. "You're looking really good."

"Thanks. I'm fine. I mean I'm doing well, thanks," he replied, stumbling over words, unable to move. He wanted to take a casual sip of champagne from the flute clasped in both hands but thought Christian might notice his hand shaking.

"How's the family?" he asked.

They had met Christian on a number of occasions, his nephew, niece, and grandmother completely transfixed by his natural charm. All except for Gemma, who had been immune.

"Gemma and the kids are fine. She's remarried now," said Anton and then felt his eyebrows drop. "Gran passed away last month."

Christian's shoulders dropped noticeably, genuinely crestfallen.

"God, Anton. I'm so sorry," he said, a familiar irritation nestling between his brows. "Why didn't you call—?"

"You changed your number. I didn't know how—" said Anton, a twinge of irritation rising, which he quickly suppressed. That wasn't strictly true either. He could have sent Christian a note to the house they once shared. "She went peacefully. In her sleep. And we gave her a good send-off. I'm sorry…."

They stood in silence for a moment, each pretending to study the artwork around them. Anton felt desolate. They stood close enough to touch, so near he could hear Christian breathing, could smell his familiar cologne that was almost a part of him. In spite of the countless intimate moments they had shared together, they addressed each other with the formality of strangers. A part of Anton wanted to reach out and pull Christian into an embrace. Another wanted to run to the gallery doors and bolt off down the street.

"So what brings you here?" said Christian, indicating the room.

"Sally. Brandon's wife," replied Anton. "Ex-colleague. What about you? I thought you hated this kind of thing."

"I'm reformed," said Christian. "Seeing anyone special?"

"More important things to do right now," he answered, trying to sound nonchalant, an attempt to mask the tremor in his voice.

"Good," said Christian, the old playful smirk Anton had missed transforming his face. "Glad I ran into you. I wanted to ask you if—"

But Christian didn't have a chance to finish, because at that moment a brawny man appeared next to him carrying two glasses of champagne. While handing one to Christian, he threw Anton an inquiring look.

"Anton, this is Max," said Christian, his smile dissolving. Max exchanged a private look with Christian, and when he turned around again Anton saw the hint of a sneer transform the man's face. Odd really, because until that moment Max appeared handsome and good natured. He didn't dress with the same care and attention as Christian—in plain denims, football shirt, and black leather jacket—but then nobody fussed over their clothes like Christian.

"So you're the famous Anton, are you?" said Max, holding out his free hand.

Anton returned the gesture and felt Max's muscular grip tighten ridiculously on his hand.

"Good to finally put a face to a name."

When Anton almost winced and yanked his hand away, he noticed Christian glaring at the floor. He could not be sure, but he thought he saw a slight shake of his head.

"Not famous," said Anton. "At least not last time I checked the headlines."

But Max turned his attention away, dropped his arm around Christian's waist, and spoke over him. "Don and Mike are in. We're now officially eight."

"Great," said Christian, nodding to the floor.

"Two more to go," said Max before turning his attention back to Anton. "How about you? Do you ski? We've got the run of a chalet in

Chamonix for a long weekend in January, haven't we? Two spaces up for grabs. You could bring a friend."

"I don't—"

But as Anton started to reply, Christian cut in. "Anton doesn't fly."

"What do you mean, 'doesn't fly'?" he said, turning to Christian and giving a quizzical look. "Why doesn't he fly?"

Anton's heart sank. He was going to say he didn't ski. Better than anyone, Christian knew the reason he didn't fly. He couldn't understand why Christian left Max's question unanswered, why he didn't volunteer an explanation.

"Personal reasons," said Anton.

"Really?" said Max with a snort. "Bit sad for a grown man. Still. Might have been a little too cozy, mightn't it? So, Chris tells me you're an art buff. What do you think of this lot?"

"Modern acrylic is not really my thing," said Anton, wondering why Christian allowed Max to abbreviate his name, something he had been vehemently against when they were together. Anton scanned the room as if to survey the artwork but in fact trying to spot Sally. He needed to be saved. "I prefer watercolor. Landscapes and seascapes. Not everyone's cup of tea."

"Nineteenth century? Like Warren or Foster? Although for my money, John Constable still takes some beating, doesn't he?" said Max, grabbing Anton's interest. The man had named a handful of his favorite artists. "And there's a painting by John Martin. What's it called? Country scene. Beautiful trees along a wide track and a—"

"*Stamner Church, Sussex*," said Anton, impressed. Of all watercolor landscapes, the man had just named his absolute favorite.

"That's the one. Nothing short of a masterpiece, isn't it?" said Max, his expression blank and unreadable. "As you know, Chris is not a fan, even though he remembered that one. Mind you, let's face it, any pretentious prick with a GCSE in art, a couple of glossy books, an Internet connection, and an ounce of intelligence can rattle off a list dead painters, can't they? Anything to make them seem more interesting."

"Max," said Christian, his voice imploring. "Please don't."

"Or what?" said Max, turning on Christian.

Anton realized too late what was happening. Max was trying to show him up in front of Christian. Embarrassed anger rose inside him. As his eyes studied the bubbles rising to the surface in his glass, wondering how to respond, he heard an unexpected voice call his name.

"Anton. There you are, my man. Thought I'd lost you" came the gentle but unexpected voice of Sean, stepping around Christian and Max.

Once stationed at Anton's side, he threw a muscled arm around his waist, and kissed him lightly on the cheek.

Anton wanted to hug the man, who stood a few inches shorter but much broader than Anton. Sexy as hell, he wore a tight-fitting black and green Paul Smith shirt opened halfway, showing off his well-defined chest and mat of short red hair. Too surprised to speak, Anton stood staring at him, mouth open.

"Well, come on," said Sean, rocking him in his grasp. "Introduce me."

"Sorry. Christian. Max. This is Sean," said Anton, noticing Christian's eyes widen as the Irishman leaned forward to clasp hands with each of the men in turn. Even Max had been thrown by Sean's sudden appearance.

"Friends of yours?" said Sean, turning to him.

"Something like that," said Anton.

"Nice to meet you both. And sorry we can't stay and chat, but I need to drag this gorgeous man away. He's in great demand tonight," said Sean before putting his large hand into Anton's and leading him through the crowd to the other side of the hall.

There in the corner of the room, Federico stood watching them approach, the fingers of one hand covering his mouth, trying to stifle a fit of giggles. Similar to Sean, he wore black jeans and an eggplant colored silk shirt open to the waist with a black vest beneath, showing off a new pendant and his chiseled chest.

"Sorry, Anton," he said. "This is my idea, not Sean's. But you did not seem to be having a good time."

"Don't you dare apologize. That's my ex with his new man," said Anton, surprising Federico with a warm hug. He felt an overwhelming gratitude to see them both. "You just saved my life. What the heck are you guys doing here?"

Sean provided a convoluted story that Anton barely kept up with about his sister being remarried to one of the featured artists' brother and how they had been invited down from Oxford to lend moral support. Federico added that he had only agreed to accompany Sean because of the free champagne. While they stood laughing together, he noticed Christian and Max leaving through the front door, in the throes of a heated argument.

"Did you call?" Sean was asking Federico when Anton returned his attention to them.

"I did. And they will be there."

"All of them?"

"Yes," said Rico with a sly grin.

"Good. We're heading to a new bar around the corner," said Sean to Anton. "And you're joining us."

"I am?" asked Anton, and then, noticing Federico's firm expression, added, "Yes, apparently I am. Let me go and say good-bye to my friend first."

Poor Sally looked worn out and started apologizing as soon as she spotted Anton. Being the gallery wife had been a lot harder than she had thought. After wishing her farewell and promising to catch up soon, he headed back across the crowded room to where Sean and Federico waited to herd him toward the doors. Outside, the chill air came as a welcome relief from the cloying warmth inside the gallery. Within minutes they were strolling, hands in pockets, along New King's Road toward Parsons Green, Federico and Sean on either side of Anton like bodyguards.

"So...," said Sean, leading them across the road at a zebra crossing. "How was the rest of your day out on the mystical moors? No relapse, I trust."

"Can you believe I stayed another night?" said Anton, and then proceeded to tell them about his stopover. When he got to the part about the phone and Stephen's car failing almost simultaneously, Sean stopped, tilted his head, and gave them an I-told-you-so expression.

"They take the piss out of me, but I'm serious. Some strange shit happens in that house," said Sean, continuing on, his head down, texting on his phone. "We're meeting friends at Arnie's, by the way. I'll get them to order us a bottle of sauvignon blanc."

"Fine with me. What did Martin mean about a ghost?" said Anton. "Have you seen one?"

"Not me," said Sean, thrusting his phone back in his jeans pocket. "Some lesbian friends of ours who came a year ago and won't go back again. They said they saw a shrouded figure in the back garden leaning against the stables, having a cigarette. But we were all pretty drunk that night, so nobody took them too seriously. Probably one of the other guests having a sly ciggie. Think the girls were more upset that someone was smoking. They told Stephen, but he just scowled, the way he does. Well, he lives there, so if anyone's going to witness something like that it would be him. Why do you ask?"

Anton decided not to tell them about the apparition in the window. "No reason," he said. "I'm like you. Intrigued by things that go bump in the night. The only midnight apparition I had in that cottage turned out to be naked and Spanish. And very much alive."

"And did you like what you saw?" said Federico, grinning, as Sean laughed aloud. "As Sean tells me, if you have got it, you must flog it."

"Flaunt it," corrected Sean, followed by another burst of laughter, as he led them into a small side road. "Not flog. Here we are."

Arnie's Bar had a facade of black paintwork and large half-frosted windows. From the outside the place appeared no larger than a normal shop. A few soft lights glowed from inside, and as Sean opened the door, Anton could see that the bar was not only deep and packed but continued on into the right-hand building. Beer-soaked sawdust, scattered across the floorboards, tainted the warm air and gave the place a welcoming atmosphere.

"Sean does not like to go to Stephen's house," said Federico, his hand pressed into the small of Anton's back, guiding him into the depths of the bar. "He says we only get invited to make up the numbers. And to keep Martin and Gallagher company."

"Used to have ten or more guests. But you've seen what hard work Stephen can be," said Sean over his shoulder, heading into the section to the right. "And he seems to be getting worse. It's like having a conversation with a statue. Can you believe that Gallagher tried to hook up the two of us? How off the mark can someone be? Before you turned up he'd barely said a word all day. Thank God you did appear, Anton, 'cause he finally had a patient to tend to, something to keep him busy."

"I don't know," said Anton, feeling the need to defend the doctor. "He's had a pretty tough time of things. And he's been nothing but kind and considerate to me."

"If you like tough love. But yeah, he did seem to take to you," said Sean, scanning the bar for a moment before waving to some people already seated at one of the bar's larger round tables and moving forward.

"You like Stephen?" said Federico, gently pushing Anton to follow Sean. Anton wasn't sure if it was a question or a statement.

"He's—" began Anton but then faltered. "Yes, I do. I know he comes across as a little rude and arrogant, but I saw another side to him over the weekend."

"Don't forget what I said. He is damaged goods, Anton" came Federico's voice in his left ear. "And anyway, we have someone we want you to meet tonight."

"Please no," said Anton, stopping and turning, horrified. "I'm not ready. Please, Rico, I'm not ready for a fix-up."

"Just to say hello," said Federico, swiveling him by the shoulders and propelling him forward. "No pressure, Anton. No proposal of marriage. You are a big boy, so just relax and enjoy yourself."

When Anton reached the table he saw two people already seated there, one a pretty young woman around Sean's age with long, straight raven hair and a pale complexion. She seemed vaguely familiar, and he wondered if she had been at the exhibition. Next to her sat an older man, possibly in his late thirties, ruggedly handsome and with a wild explosion of auburn hair. Sean was already seated next to the guy and had engaged him in conversation. When Anton caught his eye, the man nodded and smiled amiably. Absently, Anton wondered if this was the guy Federico meant him to meet. Good looking in a bohemian kind of way, he certainly piqued Anton's interest. In the meantime Federico had perched opposite the woman without a word or a sign, so he did the same.

"Bonnie, this is Anton," said Federico, placing a hand on Anton's elbow, causing the woman to stare into Anton's eyes and produce a knowing smile. Anton feared machinations were in play for which he was painfully unprepared.

"He's at the bar getting your bloody drinks order. As instructed, darling," she said to Federico while assessing Anton and holding her hand out in greeting. Her voice came out as overtly plummy, the forced poshness of those gifted or cursed with a public school education. "Fabulous to meet you."

As Anton leaned across the table to shake Bonnie's hand, he noticed Sean nudge the man next to him. Turning to Anton, he stood up and leaned across the table, holding out a hand.

"And I'm Dominic," he said, his handshake warm and friendly. By contrast, he too was educated but spoke with none of the affected embellishments of the woman. Aside from his rough appearance of ragged goatee, tousled hair, and straight-from-the-washing-machine white cotton shirt, his olive eyes smiled along with the curve of his wide mouth, playful and friendly. "So what did you think of the exhibition?"

"Some interesting pieces," said Anton, nodding and trying to sound as noncommittal as possible. In this context, the word interesting could be construed any way a person wanted.

"What Dominic is alluding to, but due to his strict public school upbringing is too polite to ask, is did you admire any of his oeuvres d'art?" said Bonnie, a wry grin on her lips.

"I'm not sure which…," he replied, frowning with confusion. Dominic continued to hold his hand in greeting, his eyes teasing, watching Anton's discomfort. His grip was firm, and Anton felt him squeeze playfully a couple of times.

"Mine stood out like a pensioner at a rave. But I noticed you hanging around them long enough," said Dominic, finally releasing Anton's hand.

"You're Collingwood? E. D. Collingwood?" asked Anton.

"Except he doesn't use the *E* any longer. Do you, Dom?" said Sean, causing Dominic to roll his eyes to the heavens. "Although don't you think Evelyn's a pretty cool name for a modern-day artist?"

"If I were female, perhaps. My grandparents claimed to be friends of Evelyn Waugh, so I inherited the name at birth. Played havoc through school," said Dominic.

"Made a man of you, my darling," said Bonnie, leaning in and kissing him on the cheek. Not a sisterly kiss either.

"So now you have to tell us something embarrassing about yourself," said Dominic, grinning playfully at Anton.

"He's a single, out of work lawyer who recently totaled his car," said Sean. "How much more do you need?"

"Ouch. Fair comment," said Dominic with a pained expression, which changed as he glanced over Anton's shoulder. "And here's Benjamin with the drinks."

As Anton began to turn, he caught Federico's wink before following everyone's stare to make out a young man heading for the table. Balanced precariously on a round tray, he had two bottles of wine and six empty glasses. Like a cat carrying her young, two large packets of potato crisps hung from his mouth. Similar to Bonnie, he had straight black hair, with a long fringe that fell over one of his dark eyes, stark against his vampiric complexion. Even dressed casually in matching navy corduroy jacket and trousers, Anton recognized him instantly.

"Ben Mercury?" said Anton as the man looked up, spat out the crisp packets, and almost dropped the tray. With Federico's help he positioned the tray at the end of the bench, almost losing one of the glasses as his startled gaze took in Anton.

"For Christ's sake, Bonnie. Are you kidding me?" said Ben, glaring at Bonnie. "Is this the chap you're trying to set me up with? If I'd known I wouldn't have forked out on the good stuff."

"See you've lost none of the old charm, Benny," said Anton, smiling pleasantly, knowing how much Ben hated that particular nickname.

"You know each other?" asked Bonnie, astonished.

"Anton bloody Swann," said Ben. "Ex-colleague. He's one of the solicitors they let go in the first cull. Stupid buggers. We worked together on a couple of cases. Shit. Pour me a large glass while I hit the little boy's room."

To describe them as having worked together was a huge overstatement. For a start, being gay was the only thing they'd ever had in common. As a paralegal, Benjamin Mercury had been assigned to work for Anton on a couple of cases and had been the bane of his life. Rude and officious to anyone in lower positions and often pulling rank where he had none, Anton inevitably had to intervene, sit him down, and caution him. He narrowly averted one incident with the pool of secretaries threatening a work-to-rule. Apart from that, he came across as overconfident and completely self-absorbed, even if he was good looking in a public schoolboy kind of way.

Anton turned to Sean and Federico and raised an eyebrow.

"Okay. My fault," said Sean, holding his hand in the air. "I told Bonnie about you. And you'd think I'd know better after what Martin and Gal did to me at the restaurant with Stephen."

"Maybe it should have been Anton there that night, not you," said Rico, nudging Sean and winking at Anton. "Then everything might have worked out for the best."

"Everything did," said Sean. "I met you, didn't I?"

Despite the initial frostiness, Anton allowed himself to relax in their company, even catching up with Ben, who had also recently been let go. As the evening wore on, as conversation drifted back to the exhibition and Anton melted into the background, the phone in his pocket beeped with a message.

Hi, Anton. This is Stephen. I hope you don't mind me contacting you. I asked Martin for your details. I wanted to apologize for rushing off from the station without saying good-bye. One of my patients panicked about her newborn's high temperature. Just wanted to thank you for your wise words and warm company, both very much appreciated. If you are ever down this way, please do pop in. It would be a pleasure to see you again. Stephen.

Saying nothing about the message to Sean or Federico, he tucked the phone back into his pocket. Unable to help himself, Anton sat back and smiled for the rest of the evening.

CHAPTER 8
NEWQUAY

ON THE last Sunday of October, Anton sat on his leather sofa with the central heating cranked up, switching his lukewarm attention between the *Financial Times* online and a midmorning cable program about modern day ghost busters. Since the unexpected weekend in Cornwall—and much like the October weather—Anton's snow-flurried life had not only settled but melted to sludge. Recruitment agents had gone quiet despite his occasional prompting, and he had begun to feel as depressed as the job market. A couple of times he toyed with the idea of replying to Stephen's text message but could think of nothing of interest to say. At around midday, as Gemma made her usual fortnightly call, he had been downloading photographs of family members taken on his mobile phone and tablet computer from the funeral weekend, as well as others taken later of the moors and the coach house.

"So," she said, straight to the point, "what news on the job front?"

No sugarcoating, no holding his hand or stroking his hair. If anyone could pull him out of a self-indulgent funk it was Gemma.

"You were right. Nobody wants to recruit before Christmas," he groaned. "I'll look more seriously after Christmas."

"I know you will," she said. "And are you managing okay?"

"I'm fine for now," he replied. She had always fretted about his finances. Personal savings, together with the small payoff from the law firm and his grandmother's bequest, could keep him going until well after Christmas, even after having to use a sizeable portion on the purchase of a secondhand BMW. His insurance monies, however, would take time coming through.

"And you're still coming for Christmas?" she asked.

"Of course I am," he replied, even though the thought of crying off and staying alone in his apartment had crossed his mind. "Where else would I go?"

"Good," she said, and sounded genuinely relieved. "So, the main reason I'm calling is because an estate agent phoned about Gran's house. Wanted to know if we intend to sell."

"Bloody hell. They don't waste any time, do they? What, do they scan the obituaries? I'd not even thought about it," said Anton, clicking systematically through the photos he had downloaded, chancing on a beautiful picture of the coach house taken from the top of a hill.

"What do you think?" he continued, following her silence. "No point leaving the place empty."

"Unless you're planning on moving back," she said and then left the words hanging.

When he caught up with her meaning, he almost laughed aloud but thought better of it.

"Nice thought, Gem, but my kind of work is here in the financial hub. And I know some people do it, but I couldn't face that long a commute every day."

And as much as he loved his sister and her kids, he could not imagine being near them twenty-four seven. Even in his present situation, he enjoyed his own space too much.

"I know," she said with a soft snort. "Worth a try, though. But if we're going to sell, we'll need to empty the place."

Clearing the home of their grandmother's furniture and belongings, as well as their own from when they'd lived there, had not even crossed his mind. But she was right; they would have to do it at some point. Right then his silence must have prompted her to speak again.

"I'd go over myself, but Ewan's got an executive training course in Scotland this week, and I've got my hands full with the kids off for half term. He found an ad in the local paper for home clearance companies that will come in and—"

"No," he said, cutting her off. "I don't want strangers poking through her things. She deserves better than that. Look, I'm not exactly rushed off my feet at the moment, so how about I come down and stay. Spend some time with you and the kids while they're on school holidays. We could go over to Gran's during the day to clear things out, or I can go myself and see you in the evenings."

"Would you?" said Gemma, brightening. "Anton, that would be wonderful. And the kids would love to see you. Are you absolutely sure?"

"Yes," he said, breathing out a sigh of surrender. He owed her that much after his behavior at the end of his previous visit. More importantly, her new husband, Ewan, would not be there. "Give me a chance to give the car a good run too. How about I drive down tomorrow?"

Which is what they agreed, and the next morning he set off on the long, familiar route. Planning to meet her at their grandmother's house at two thirty, he arrived an hour earlier than anticipated so decided to drive around town for old time's sake. Apart from generic housing estates and the questionable pedestrianization of part of the town center, Newquay had changed little since Anton's childhood. At least that's how he remembered it. Finally on his way to the house, he couldn't resist a quick diversion along the seafront, overlooking the wild gray ocean and spume-topped waves, before heading out along Cliff Road. Newquay had a charm all year round, but for Anton, winter months held treasured memories and magic, when tourists had scurried back to the warmth of their inland homes or back to their more temperate countries.

Gemma and Ewan lived to the north of Newquay, away from the town center, in a small community of identical new-build properties. By contrast, built in the 1900s, their grandparents' house of gray granite stood proudly individual from others along the terrace. Built on a hill in the older part of town, the back of the house overlooked a golf course bordering the vast sea beyond. Anton had only visited a few times since leaving for university, but the building evoked mixed memories. Standing outside the front gate waiting for his sister and her kids, he was reminded of their childhood: the mad morning dashes down the hill to catch the school bus, the temperamental lock on the front gate that his grandmother habitually reminded him to close properly, the small patch of front garden that had been his domain after their granddad passed on, the same curtains in the front living room windows that he remembered as a child, now drab and faded with age. Funny how a building could elicit as many feelings as the memory of a loved one.

Gemma turned up fifteen minutes after him. She beamed a self-satisfied smile when she saw him and pecked him on the cheek. Anton half suspected her mention of the house clearance service had been a ploy to get him to come down. Not that he minded in the least. He would have only spent the week back in Croydon doing next to nothing.

"Maybe I should tackle the outside first."

"Tell you what. Why don't you get the kids to see if there's anything worth keeping from the garden shed. It's where Gran kept most of our old games and toys," said Anton as Gemma unlocked the front door and stepped inside. "Then you can tackle Gran's bedroom upstairs. Open the window and you can keep an eye on them."

Anton had not anticipated how long the clearance would take or how difficult it would be. This was partly because his nephew and niece were more of a hindrance than a help, constantly running in and asking him or Gemma about one tatty object or another. At least they kept the mood light, their laughter a welcome sound ringing throughout the otherwise silent house. Another reason, something his sister shared when they showed one another items for either dumping or keeping, was the difficulty in throwing out things that had once been special: an old patchwork blanket their grandmother had knitted and used to keep them warm on long car journeys, his grandfather's collection of tobacco pipes, the old wooden elephant foot that used to house their array of umbrellas. By Tuesday afternoon, they had amassed a pile of "not sure" items and combed through, being brutally selective. More than the physical aspect of the task, the few days had been emotionally draining. By Tuesday evening, they had broken the back of the chore. Both had taken what they wanted, loading up

Anton's car, while other manageable items had been dropped off at the local charity shop, according to their late grandmother's wishes. Earlier in the afternoon, the shop's van took away the bulky furniture, much still in good if not pristine condition, leaving the house an empty shell. If not for his grandmother's express wishes, he might have used the opportunity to call Martin and ask him to inspect some of the older pieces. On Wednesday morning Gemma left him alone to go through the few remaining cupboards upstairs in his former bedroom.

Standing in the center of the bare room, he scanned the walls, the space appearing huge without furniture, with yellowing patches on the wallpaper where pictures or posters used to hang. Even now, the room smelled vaguely the same as he remembered, a musky teenage scent mixed with oil paints and turpentine. He had been happy there, despite the tragic circumstances that led to them being brought up by their grandparents. In this very room, he had first kissed another boy during a game of truth or dare. Four of his school friends from the local coed had come home with him, two girls and two other boys. One of them was his best friend, Jimmy, and the other was Trevor Hobbs, the boyfriend of Janie. Sitting cross-legged in a circle on the bedroom floor, Trevor had asked for a dare. Janie's friend Alison had dared him to kiss Anton. Bigger and more popular than all of them, Trevor played the position of goalkeeper for the school football team. When Alison first announced the dare Anton had been horrified and protested loudly. Trevor, egged on by the others, came over and sat in front of him. Anton remembered the feeling of acute anxiousness and how he had grabbed a cushion from the bed and hugged the soft material into his stomach. With a playful grin, Trevor leaned in and whispered to Anton, encouraging him to give the audience a show. Anton nodded and went with the kiss, which was slow and stagey, like a movie kiss done more for effect than anything meaningful. But for Anton, the kiss had rocked his world, and he had barely heard the sound of the girls' squealed laughter and Jimmy's groan of disgust. As Trevor finally pulled away, still grinning, and to the applause of the girls, Anton had to quickly transfer the cushion to his lap.

Now this room would soon belong to someone else, perhaps another child who would cultivate his or her own memories. All the dreams he had dreamed, the lives he had wished for himself, the secret yearnings and longings he had felt, were all associated with this room. But as he had learned from an early age with the death of his parents, everything in the world is transient, and we can only hope our time is well spent. And most importantly, those dreams and longings become a part of you, not of a place, and they go with you wherever you go. To scatter the thoughts away, he shook his head and reached for the handle of the cupboard door.

Behind a pile of tattered board games and a rucksack that had seen better days, he found his old painting materials, all carefully stored and arranged together. For sentimental reasons perhaps, his grandmother had kept them, along with a number of his paintings. Among the equipment, he lifted out a stack of unused cold-pressed papers, his large enamel tin of forty-eight different shades of paint, the round paint-speckled biscuit tin containing tubes of new and used oil paints, assorted rounded sponges, and the wooden easel his grandfather had built for him out of scraps of old wood. Still on the top shelf stood the cedarwood box his grandmother had proudly found in a jumble sale to store his assortment of brushes, and next to that a pack of charcoals for sketching. Not only did he not have the heart to throw any of them away, but the mere sight lifted his spirits. After boxing everything he wanted and placing the equipment in his car boot, he called Gemma to let her know he had finished. While waiting for her to pick up, he turned back to the house, and a great sadness hit him. As a final act he walked over and made sure the front gate was latched properly.

"Gem," he asked, after chatting briefly. "Do you mind if I set up my paints in the spare room?"

While waiting for her response, a message pinged onto his phone. When he pulled the device to his face, he smiled to see Martin's name on the display and the beginnings of a long text. Putting the phone back to his ear, he missed part of what Gemma was saying.

"…door closed if you're painting nudes. And as long as you open a window. What brought this on? Feeling inspired?"

"You could say that. Okay, I'm going to head home now and set up my easel. Takeaway tonight?"

"Let's talk later. I'm about to start yoga class. Phones are a no-no."

"Where are the kids?"

"They have a crèche here. Speak to you at home."

Sitting in the warmth of the BMW, Anton's spirits lifted on reading the message from Martin, which rambled on about him and Gallagher passing by Croydon the coming Saturday on their way back from Gallagher's elderly parents in Coulsdon. Martin ended by suggesting they meet up for an early dinner or a quick drink in Croydon, only if Anton was free. Anton fired back an immediate response, accepting the invite and suggesting a popular local bistro, which more importantly had free parking at the back.

That night he stayed awake past midnight mulling over his lukewarm life, his hands thrust behind his head, staring at the ceiling. Thanks to Martin's message, he finally shook the morose mood by recalling the events of the weekend he had spent on the moor with people he now regarded as friends. Add to that his chance meeting with Sean and Federico and planned weekend rendezvous with Martin and Gallagher, together with the message from Stephen that he had saved to read from time to time, and he felt much better. Exhausted but with no sign of sleep on the horizon, he decided to get up and paint. His habit had always been to work from his own photographs or sketches. Sitting in his pajamas, he decided to use the media on his tablet computer, photos he had downloaded, his heart drawn to the snap of the coach house. Nothing about the photo needed to be changed or embellished, the shot so beautifully clear—a balanced composition with sharp contrasting colors—it hardly needed recreating in watercolors. But Anton felt a rare inspiration and decided to follow his instincts. By the time he noticed the orange-blue dawn staining the horizon beyond the bedroom window, he had already produced the beginnings of a satisfying reproduction.

Late to the breakfast table that morning, he sensed Gemma studying him while he poured himself coffee. Oddly enough the children were nowhere to be seen, and Anton assumed they were either in the garden playing—although he could hear nothing—or were already out somewhere.

"When do you plan on heading back?"

"Saturday morning."

"You don't want to stay the weekend?"

"Can't, Gem. Got an important errand to run," he said. At least he hoped so, as long as he could get a decent frame for his painting. "And I'm meeting up with friends on Saturday night."

"Your new friends?" she asked, her approval obvious. "Good for you. Sounds like they're a lot of fun."

"They are."

Cradling his hands around the coffee mug, he raised his tired eyes and smiled at her. Martin and Gallagher were just the remedy he needed to get over the emotional roller coaster the week had provided.

"You look shattered. Didn't you sleep last night?" she asked.

"Not much. Does it show?"

"And how."

She let it go, but he could see her checking on him from time to time. While he took a large and much needed swallow of coffee, she scanned the recipe books on a shelf in the kitchen.

"Ewan will be back tomorrow, so I thought we'd have a family dinner together. I'm going to push the boat out and do the rack of lamb with honey mint from the Patrice Legrande cookbook. Kids aren't overfond of lamb, but Ewan will love it. What do you think?"

"Sounds great," said Anton, smiling at her but without much enthusiasm.

"You're okay with lamb?" she asked, locating and plucking the book from the shelf before turning to him.

"Fine."

"Okay, little brother," she said, thumping the book down on the kitchen table in front of him and startling him. "Spit it out. What's eating away at you?"

"Nothing. Everything. Can't get past what a bloody awful year this has been. What with Gran, losing the job, totaling my car, and—everything," he said, purposely excluding Christian from the hit list. "And now, to add insult to injury, emptying out and selling off the house we grew up in. Feels like doors are slamming all around. I'm just wondering when things are going to start getting better."

"What have I told you about wallowing?" she said, leaning over and tapping him on the tip of the nose with her forefinger, the way she did with her children. "Stop worrying and focus on the positives. Like I've told you a hundred times, things happen for a reason. You have a snazzy, more reliable car now, you've got your own apartment, and you've made some nice new friends. Before you know it, you'll be up to your neck in work and bemoaning the fact that you need more time off. After that everything else will fall into place."

"Soon, I hope. Simply for sanity's sake."

"Do me a favor, though, Ant."

"What's that?"

"Don't jump at the first thing that comes along. Consider what *you* want before making a decision."

Tired as he was, Anton had to smile at his sister's comment. When he met her eyes, he flicked a salute, which had her rolling her eyes. Soon after that she started bustling about the kitchen, grabbing at her car keys.

"Right. I need to get going."

"Where are the kids?"

"They have a swimming lesson this morning. Cheryl from down the road took them. I'm going to meet them now. Want to tag along?"

"If it's okay with you, I'm going to potter around town first thing this morning, before the rush. Maybe have lunch out. Get a nice bottle of wine for dinner tomorrow and a cake for dessert. Then I thought I'd come back and do some more painting."

"Well, you've got your key, so come and go as you please. And Anton?"

"Yes," he replied, looking up.

"Cheer up, will you?"

Driving into town early had been a wise choice. Two of the shops he entered had barely opened for the day, and he could browse freely. One of those, a charity shop, had a pitiful front window of two contorted Styrofoam mannequins in drab dresses of powder lavender and powder lemon, complete with African tribal jewelry. He almost passed by. But on a whim he decided to enter and, after a brief browse, found exactly what he was looking for. The portrait of a lone horseman had faded to transparence, colors barely discernible. But the frame—what really caught Anton's attention—was perfect, golden lacquer overlaid with burnished vines and leaves. At first glance the structure appeared stained, but held up to the light, Anton could see the frame just needed a simple cleanup. After pulling the measuring tape from his pocket to check the dimensions—even though he knew instinctively it was right—he took the picture to the counter. When the old woman running the store demanded ten pounds, he rubbed his chin for a moment before offering five. They settled on eight pounds, and Anton walked away with the newspaper-wrapped picture tucked under his arm. By eleven thirty he had everything he wanted and, feeling pleased with himself, stopped off in a local pub for a ploughman's lunch and a pint of real ale. Even though the fare filled a hole, neither the ale nor the meal could match those he had enjoyed so much at the Hawk's Tavern.

On Friday afternoon, after spending the morning cleaning and successfully fixing the landscape onto the frame, Anton had been so immersed in another painting—this time using oils—that he did not notice the sizeable bulk stopping by his bedroom door.

"Anton" came the deep Welsh voice. "Gemma told me you were staying the week."

He peered up from the behind the canvas to see Ewan hovering in the doorway. At least this time he was fully clothed. In fact, not only did he fill out the navy suit really well, he looked every part the professional.

"My goodness. You scrub up well. How was the course?"

Ewan grinned almost shyly.

"Edinburgh. Bloody cold, but the program was okay. High performing teams and all that nonsense. They kept me back a day to discuss arrangements for a national piss-up for all managers in December. And because they've decided to hold it in my neck of the woods, guess who gets lumbered with the local arrangements?"

They exchanged a few more tentative pleasantries, but Anton could tell Ewan wanted to say more, was building up the nerve to speak his piece. Anton dreaded what that might be.

"Thing is, Gemma's making dinner tonight. And I wondered if you wanted to grab a beer before? Head down the local. In a couple of hours' time. They'll be showing the game."

Anton put down his paintbrush. So that was it. Gemma had also been badgering Ewan about making more of an effort with her brother. Perhaps, he thought, it was time they had a talk.

"Look, Ewan, why don't you come in and shut the door?"

"Oh. God, no," said Ewan, his face panic-stricken. "It's okay. I—I'm fine here. Don't want to disturb, and all that. And the smell's a bit strong, see? Don't know how you can stand it."

Sudden realization almost had Anton laughing out loud. How could he have misjudged the situation so badly? The doorframe had been Ewan's boundary. Even in his naked state, he had never ventured any farther into the room. Anton wondered if he had even been aware of his nudity. Probably not, or certainly not something he would have cared about. Him and his other straight football chums spent time naked in each other's company—in the changing rooms after a game or in the communal splash pool—and thought nothing of it. But now Ewan acted like a frightened child when asked to come into the room and shut them in.

"Force of habit, I suppose. I love the smell of paint," said Anton, smiling and relaxing. "Reminds me of being young again and getting my first paint set."

"Nice," said Ewan, clearly not interested. "So how about a couple of pints? A bit later on?"

Anton folded his arms and took a deep breath, wondering how to deal with the man. Poor Ewan appeared almost terrified, and if Gemma had anything to do with his request, then he had every right to be.

"Look, Ewan. You have a sister, don't you?"

"Susie, yeah."

"Does she ever drink? When she goes out? You know, alcohol."

"Yeah, 'course she does," said Ewan, baffled. "White wine. Or sometimes one of them fancy cocktails."

"Wine's good. And what sport does she like?"

"Dunno. Tennis, s'pose. Caught her watching men's diving at the Olympics."

"Perfect. So if you want to have a night out, think of me as a sister. Or sister-in-law, if that makes more sense."

"Oh," said Ewan, grappling with the thought before reality dawned on him. "Oh, I see. So you don't like rugby, then?"

"Ah. Actually, yes, I love rugby," said Anton. "I thought you meant football. Not a big fan, I'm afraid."

"Got it. Rugby league and chardonnay? Best not take you down the boozer, then. Not sure the two should be seen together."

At that remark Anton peered over to see Ewan's quizzical expression and burst into laughter. Almost instantly the big man brightened up at his own joke and joined in the laughter.

"Let me get a bottle or two from the corner shop. I'll get myself a pack of Kilkenny, if that's all the same to you. Game's on at five. We can watch it in the den."

"Brilliant. And look, I could really do with your opinion here. Leave the door open. I'm painting a picture from a snap I took of the kids in Gran's back garden."

Tentatively, Ewan moved across the room and stood by Anton's left shoulder. His slight intake of breath told Anton that he had not expected to see what he now witnessed.

"You can see the picture on my tablet computer. But I've tried messing with the light, to brighten things up and make it look like a summer's day. Tuesday here started out great but quickly turned gray and miserable."

"Anton, that is amazing," whispered Ewan, lightly patting Anton's shoulder.

Absently, Anton realized the intimate gesture was the first they had shared, apart from the occasional and awkward handshake in greeting or farewell.

"Gemma's right, you've a real talent there. She'll love it."

"Good. Let me finish off here and clean up. Then after I've packed my bags, I'll join you for the game."

"You not staying the weekend?"

"No. I need to get back, and I've got an errand to run Saturday morning. Something I should have done a while ago. Then I'm meeting friends in the afternoon."

"Fair enough," said Ewan, heading back to the door but then stopping and turning at the safe open doorway. "Oh, and you might want to check that phone of yours. Wasn't being nosy, but there's a couple of missed calls by the looks of things."

All three calls were from an unknown caller, but on the last someone had left a voice message. Something seemed different in the all too familiar voice, a vulnerability Anton had never heard before.

Anton, where the hell are you? I need to talk to you.

The initial irritation in the tone softened as the message continued.

I—um—I dropped by your flat earlier today, but you weren't in. Either that or you weren't answering. I don't know. Look, I'm going to be in town tomorrow. On my own. Thought we could have a drink at the Fisherman's Wharf along the river in Hammersmith. For old time's sake. Say around eight o'clock. Please come. I really need to speak to you.

Um, this is Christian.

CHAPTER 9
GIFTS

EARLY SATURDAY lunchtime traffic heading out of Newquay flowed far better than Anton had anticipated. Holiday weekenders must have written off the idea of getting away following a depressing November week of fierce winds and icy rain, a precursor perhaps to a bitter winter to come. But an early morning downpour had passed and given way to unfettered sunshine. In fact, Anton had made such good progress that he almost missed the hidden turnoff from the A30.

After glancing at the dashboard clock, he signaled and turned into the lane. Fifteen minutes out of his schedule would do no harm, he decided; a short errand before he hit the road for home. Maintenance work and other holdups aside, he would still be back comfortably by six thirty and ready to meet up with Christian at eight. Perhaps not comfortably. Even now his heart wavered at the thought of Christian's mysterious yet insistent voice message, something he forced himself not to overthink. In his heart he knew he should be feeling remorse about cancelling on Martin and Gallagher, whose cheery reply had been, "No problem, old man. Another time."

In daylight he had no trouble finding the route to the coach house, and even remembered the landmarks—the sentinel hedgerows concealing everything beyond, the sudden crossroads, the long straight lane with drystone walling cutting through the moorlands like the binding through a book—that would eventually lead to the coach house. Everything looked unthreatening and picturesque in the sunshine, a very different journey from the one he had taken a month earlier.

As he approached the cottage, his heart sank at the sight of something he should have expected. An unsightly new addition.

The For Sale signpost of a regional estate agent in loud blue and red font had been fixed to one side of the front gate. Somehow the placard cheapened the setting and gave the cozy building an air of obsolescence, of impending abandonment.

After performing a three-point turn in the narrow lane and stopping outside the front gate, he climbed out of the BMW. Unlike the last occasion when he had stumbled on the cottage, he felt grateful to see no signs of life, no parked Range Rover or lights inside the building. Without fuss he could leave the gifts on the front step and make a quick exit. He propped open the gate and strode the few short steps to the oak door, but then glimpsed a field gate open to his right beyond the garden wall perimeter, one he had not noticed previously. Martin had mentioned stables at the back of the property, so out of curiosity Anton wandered along the length of the front garden to check. There, next to a track leading to the back of the property, parked under a lean-to shelter out of sight of the road, sat Stephen's racing-green Rover.

Initially thoughts of creeping back to the door, dropping the gift off discreetly, and speeding away filled him, but another, undoubtedly a reflection of his grandmother's sense of correctness, told him to check whether anyone was home. The least he could do after not responding to Stephen's text message. After glancing through a window into the empty dining room on his way back, he knocked hard on the front door and waited. On this occasion he decided one attempt would suffice. When, after a couple of minutes, nobody came to the door, he sighed with a relieved breath he hadn't realized he was holding and bent down to place the bag on the doormat.

"And to what do I owe the pleasure?" came the voice of Stephen from behind him.

Anton groaned inwardly. Taking a deep breath, he plastered on a happy face before turning to address the man standing at the gate. For a second his smile faltered. Decked out in a tight gray sports vest and black silk shorts, with chest rising and falling, the doctor had clearly just finished a run. Anton tore his gaze away from the glisten of sweat on the man's broad shoulders and muscular chest. Opening the gate, Stephen appeared to be in good spirits and seemed genuinely pleased to see him.

"You caught me. I've come bearing gifts. A small gesture of thanks," said Anton, indicating the bag in his hand. "Hopefully in lieu of a sizeable medical bill."

"You want to come inside?" said Stephen, ignoring the comment and chuckling misty breath into the chill early afternoon air.

"Certainly," said Anton, checking his watch. Even if fifteen minutes turned into half an hour, he could still make good time on his return. "For a little while."

"Good," he said, unlocking the front door. "I'll put the kettle on."

Once inside Stephen led Anton to a room on the left of the front of the house, a spacious sitting room, one he had not entered during his previous visit. A large red brick fireplace built into the end commanded the room, surrounded by worn brown leather settees and easy chairs arranged around a small oak coffee table. Unlit logs filled the grate, but even so the house already felt warm and cozy, testament to an efficient central heating system carefully hidden away.

"Give me a few minutes," he said at the door. "And make yourself at home."

To keep himself distracted Anton inspected the room. Two honey oak bookcases either side of the chimney had an assortment of medical and other reading materials. Interspersed in spaces on the shelves of each bookcase sat small bronze and silver sculptures of faces and figurines and framed photographs.

After scanning the top two shelves of book titles, pulling a few off to examine but understanding none of the medical terminology, he picked up and studied one of two silver-framed photographs. The first showed Stephen with his arm around a man he assumed to be Sebastian, both in dress suits, but Sebastian wearing tennis pumps instead of formal evening shoes. He stood a few inches shorter than Stephen, similar to Anton's height, and had a playfulness about him, as though he had been told a joke and was trying hard not to laugh aloud. Returning the frame to the shelf, Anton instantly liked Sebastian and how he appeared much less somber than Stephen: good looking in a relaxed way and a nice complement to the handsome seriousness of the doctor.

The other photograph showed Stephen's family together. Dressed also for a formal function, Stephen's mother and father stood in the middle with a much younger Stephen on one side and a red-cheeked Susanna, his sister, on the other. Everyone held a champagne flute, looking relaxed and happy, no doubt a little tipsy, laughing at a shared joke. Anton could see how much Stephen resembled his father, the same stance, the same solid and handsome features.

"My parents' twenty-fifth wedding anniversary," said Stephen. Anton turned to see Stephen setting down two mugs onto mats on the coffee table. "Towards the end of the evening. As you can probably tell."

"It's lovely," said Anton wistfully, carefully placing the photograph back on the shelf. Folding his arms, he continued to look at the happy scene, wondering briefly if his own family would have been as close had his mother and father been alive still.

"How's your father?" he asked, turning around and seeing the doctor seated across the room, a towel around his neck, his muscular thighs straddling the arm of the settee.

"He's doing fine. Back home now, to the relief of the ward nurses," said Stephen, a crease appearing between his brows. "Fortunately no paralysis. But he needs constant care, and mum's not really up to it. I've organized a private nurse for him. And I get there as often as work allows."

An awkward silence fell that Anton felt unable to fill; he simply grinned grimly and nodded. When he reached for his mug, Stephen followed suit, and both men sipped tea in contemplative quiet. Eventually Stephen broke the spell.

"So what have you been up to?" he asked.

"Not much. I spent the week in Newquay clearing out my grandmother's house," said Anton, "getting the place ready to sell. I thought it would be easy. But there are so many happy memories. I've got a car boot full of things I couldn't bring myself to toss out."

"I understand completely," said Stephen, his smile fading. "But you will. Eventually. In your own time, when you're ready."

"God, I'm sorry," said Anton, realizing Stephen must have had to go through the same ritual with Sebastian's things. "I'm forgetting."

"Don't be," said Stephen. "Grief is a process we all work through in our own way. And I hear you've had more than your fair share for one lifetime."

Anton fell silent. He felt the previous mood of the man slipping away so made a point of changing the subject.

"Did you hear I met Sean and Federico in town? At an art exhibition, of all places."

Stephen had not heard, so Anton went on to tell him about finding them both sipping champagne, saving him from his ex and the new partner, and then Sean's disastrous attempt to try and fix him up with someone who turned out to be an ex-colleague. He felt sure he saw the doctor's smile slip briefly at the mention of the fix-up, but by the time Anton had reached the end of the story, he had Stephen laughing aloud.

"Okay, so come on, then. What did you bring me?" asked Stephen, arms folded, tilting his head to the bag discarded on the floor.

"Look. It's nothing much," said Anton. He reached down and brought out the first small pack, already feeling guilty at the trifling amount he had spent on the presents. "A couple of small things."

Across from him, Stephen sat grinning at him. Anton found himself relaxing, enjoying the return of the doctor's good humor.

"I found this in a shoe repair shop, of all places. It's Bakelite cleaner. To spruce up those electrical fixtures before you get any potential buyers poking around the place. Maybe even give that old phone of yours a makeover."

Anton tossed the present to Stephen, who quickly unfolded his arms and caught the tin before scanning the instructions.

"And this," said Anton, pulling the CD from his bag, "is a copy of the jazz compilation you mentioned. At least I think it's the one. The songs have been remastered, and the sound quality is excellent.

The woman whose voice you were all admiring is Mimi Perrin, a song called *Naima* by John Coltrane. This I found in a second hand record store in Newquay."

Again he tossed the object to Stephen. On this occasion Stephen's smile drained away as he examined the cover. Anton bit his lip at his stupidity, wondering how he could have been so insensitive. But Stephen's smile reappeared as he gazed over at Anton.

"This is the one. I recognize the artwork," he said, nodding, his voice soft with emotion. "And of course it's Mimi Perrin. Really thoughtful."

Relieved, Anton pulled his final gift from the bag. He had wrapped the rectangular item in brown paper, which he proceeded to rip away while Stephen continued to study the CD cover. Satisfied, he positioned the small painting on the far end of the settee for Stephen to view and then stepped back.

"The coach house?" whispered Stephen, getting up and standing next to him.

"Painted by a lesser known artist. Yours truly. I've even signed in the bottom right corner. You never know, if I don't get a job soon, I might have to resort to painting for a living. And if I become famous it might be worth a bit of money when I kick the bucket," he said, laughing to himself and admiring his work. Anton wasn't sure if it had something to do with the light in the room, but he felt pleased at how he had captured the essence of the building and surroundings, one of his better pieces. "So even if you don't own the cottage anymore, you can still keep a memory. And it's small enough to fit in your suitcase, if you want to hang it in your tent in Africa, or wherever they—"

But Anton didn't have a chance to finish.

While he had been rambling on, Stephen's gaze had fallen upon him. Turning to face him now, the doctor stepped in and placed his hands either side of Anton's face the way he had the first time they met, but this time kissed him firmly. Anton was taken by surprise, almost stumbled back a step, until he recovered enough to thrust himself into the embrace. His mind reeled, woken from blindness, his heart hammering, suddenly alive to the attraction that had been simmering for the doctor.

When Stephen's tongue pushed against his teeth, he opened his mouth willingly and welcomed him. Coiling his arms around Stephen's waist, he pulled their bodies tightly together. Damp with perspiration, his torso felt lean and hard with muscle and trembled as their bodies meshed together.

Stephen pushed away first, breathing deeply. Lust-darkened blue eyes gazed hungrily into Anton's as he appeared to make up his mind. Lifting the lapels of Anton's jacket, he pulled them wide and shoved them backward. The coat dropped from his shoulders onto the floor. Immediately he grabbed a fistful of Anton's white polo shirt, pulled him forward, and kissed him again. Without letting go of the shirt, he began to walk backward, leading him out of the room toward the stairs. Both of them tripped on steps, removing items of clothing in their haste to reach the bedroom. Inside, they embraced again, both bare chested and breathing heavily. Anton stood in his underpants, Stephen in running shorts and white socks, the nipples on his carved, hairless chest as erect as standing stones.

While Anton stood with his back to the bed, Stephen withdrew his lips and breathed something meaningless into Anton's left ear before gently kissing and licking the lobe. Then, with slow deliberation, so that Anton's skin trembled at each delicate touch, he trailed his fingertips and hot, damp mouth down Anton's chin, his throat, and into the cluster of dark hairs on his chest. While teasing Anton's left nipple with his tongue and nipping gently with his teeth, sending delicious shivers through him, Stephen's hands trailed down to his waist, gripped the band of his underwear, and gently eased them down, Anton's already rigid cock springing to attention.

Anton gasped softly and squeezed his eyes closed. Instantly the doctor dropped to the floor, his hot breath caressing Anton's genitals, his hand wrapped around the shaft, then pulling back the foreskin. Sudden, moist heat enveloped him as a hot mouth closed over the bulbous head of his manhood, the doctor's tongue repeatedly circling and teasing the purple rim. Anton held his breath, but when Stephen took the whole length into his throat and cupped his balls in one sure movement, Anton moaned aloud and almost lost his balance. He had not felt such raw pleasure in far too long.

While Anton wove his hands into the head of blond hair below him, Stephen's mouth began rhythmically riding him, using long, hungry strokes, taking him deep into his gullet, his hands clutching and kneading Anton's upper thighs and buttocks. Slowly, almost imperceptibly, Stephen increased the speed of each lunge until Anton lost himself and began instinctively pushing into each glorious thrust, the furnace building in his stomach and around his thighs. Arousal had begun to turn into orgasm—he had not come in such a long time—and he caught himself before hitting the point of no return.

"Uhn, Stephen, I—" he whimpered urgently and left the rest to the doctor.

Stephen understood instinctively; he pulled his mouth away and, with one hand, squeezed the base of Anton's shaft tightly near the balls, leaving Anton gasping and bereft but averting a premature climax. At the same time, he heard the doctor frantically wrenching open and closing drawers in his bedside cupboard before appearing to find what he sought. On his feet, he confronted Anton again, their faces barely an inch apart, sharing each other's hot breath.

"Beautiful," whispered the doctor, kissing him again, his tongue flickering through Anton's mouth, sharing his essence.

Still facing Stephen, Anton sat down abruptly on the edge of the bed and carefully pulled down the doctor's shorts. Stephen's uncut cock sprang out monumentally from his bush of blond hair, the thick shaft curving upward, the mauve head poking through the foreskin, engorged and battle ready. Anton placed his hands around the man's waist and then brought them down in a caress over his hairy thighs, savoring the change in texture, bringing them slowly in closer to massage his sac and quivering shaft. Stephen had braced a hand on Anton's shoulder and bent to kiss the top of his head. Anton reciprocated by closing his mouth around the whole length, holding his breath, and taking him deep inside, squeezing a blissful moan from Stephen. He wondered if Stephen had also not ejaculated recently or was simply already on the verge of coming, because after several mouthfuls of his long hot shaft, he pulled Anton's head away and knelt down again.

With Anton sitting on the bed, his cock straining to his navel, Stephen used one hand to gently push him back flat onto the bed before grabbing the back of each knee, lifting his legs in the air, and pushing them backward toward his head. Rising then, he carefully parted Anton's legs and pulled a pillow to place beneath his lower back.

Hot breath caressed his backside, sending shivers through him as the doctor's mouth kissed his buttocks and then trailed his tongue into the crevice. Pushing hard and damp with saliva, he probed deeper, the stubble from his chin prickling him, the stiff tongue loosening the muscles of Anton's hole and sending ripples of unrivalled pleasure shuddering through him. Anton moaned aloud with loss as Stephen finally took his mouth away.

Using his forefinger and the cool lube he had taken from a drawer, Stephen began to massage the area around his rosebud, sending tremors through Anton until he could feel the hotness in his muscles subsiding, allowing Stephen to probe one and then two fingers into his cavity. Anton willed himself to surrender to the doctor's expert hand, invasive but sensual, even though his own erection subsided. Slowly and expertly, Stephen continued, coaxing the muscled wall to expand, probing deeper into Anton's body until he became hard again and almost cried out for the next inevitable pleasure.

And Stephen was ready for him. While one of his hands had set about preparing Anton, the other had rolled a condom and a liberal coating of lube onto his own manhood. He withdrew his fingers then and dropped on top of Anton, his muscled arms either side of Anton's head, the tip of Stephen's large member knocking on the rim of his entrance. As he waited, Stephen's gaze burned deep into Anton, and he raised his eyebrows in a silent question. Anton responded with a loving smile and a gentle nod. The moment of absolute trust between two men, between two warriors going together into battle.

While Anton inhaled deeply, Stephen's hips moved forward, his cock sliding past the first soft, muscled boundary. By careful degrees,

Stephen pushed farther and farther, while hot pain blossomed and then subsided for Anton. Once his whole shaft lay inside, Stephen stilled and kissed him passionately.

Taking a deep breath, Stephen pushed his upper torso away and, one at a time, pulled Anton's ankles into place on each of his shoulders. Satisfied, he withdrew his shaft but stopped before pulling out completely. With a grunt of carnal pleasure, he began pumping his hips rhythmically, hammering his full length into Anton with long, slow strokes. As the momentum increased, Anton began pushing into the lunges, meeting him partway, which produced gasps of pleasure from Stephen, who in turn increased the speed and pressure.

After clasping Stephen's upper arms to keep himself anchored, Anton sensed his own cock vying for attention, and while the bed creaked and groaned with their exertions, he grabbed his shaft and began to pump furiously. Immersed in the pleasure, Anton's body shuddered to the assault on his senses, the pounding of his prostate, the fire building in his stomach and flanks, until this time, his buttocks clenched tight as he allowed the orgasm to rise from him. Arching his back, he opened his mouth wide and emitted a moan of abandoned joy as the first wave of pleasure erupted and a jet of hot juice spurted from his cock into the dark hair of his chest. He heard Stephen gasp too and murmur something he could not discern because the next rapturous upsurge had already begun to thunder through his body.

While Anton shuddered with pleasure and wrung out the last drops of seed, Stephen's strokes had become faster, more erratic and less evenly spaced. The eyes hovering above Anton squeezed shut, the face contorted in ecstasy. In a swift, practiced movement, Stephen withdrew from him, ripped the condom from his cock, straddled Anton, and emptied the load onto his chest, squirting rivers of hot nectar into the pool already left there.

Finally expended, Stephen collapsed onto Anton, breathing heavily and hotly in his ear, the full weight of his spent body on top. They lay that way for a good while, until it felt as though their hearts were beating in sync. At one point Anton wondered if Stephen had fallen asleep.

"Shower," Stephen whispered eventually into Anton's ear as he unglued their chests and rose from the bed.

Anton watched the taut backside disappear into the room at the back of the bedroom. He lay there wondering what he should do. For too long he had been out of practice, no longer knew the rules of the game. Was this a sign for him to clean up as best he could, get dressed, and leave without disturbing the host, like one of many sordid late-night encounters during his college years? Or should he wait, as with Christian, until one had finished showering, and then the other could take his turn? And if so, would Stephen also behave as if nothing had happened, as though they had simply expended energy after physical exertion? While he lay staring at the ceiling, Stephen's voice came from the doorway.

"You coming or not?"

Anton didn't need to be asked twice.

The shower proved far more intimate than their first intense encounter. Even though so much needed to be said, barely a word was spoken. Unhurried and sensual, both men explored the other's body, lathering soap over muscles and into crevices, stopping from time to time to kiss deeply. Before long, both men were aroused, and this time Stephen took their lathered cocks in his hand and brought them off in a shuddering climax.

"No idea what it is about this place, but I seem to have difficulty leaving," said Anton, toweling himself off in the bedroom and smirking at Stephen. "Or perhaps I do."

"Stay for dinner," said Stephen, in the process of pulling on a pair of gray track bottoms. "Or do you need to rush back?"

"Shit," said Anton, freezing, remembering his promised meet-up with Christian and how angry his ex-boyfriend could become if Anton arrived late. He managed to catch himself, smiling apologetically at Stephen. "I want to stay, more than anything. I just—I'd arranged to meet a friend."

"That's fine. If you've made other plans," began Stephen.

"No, it's not!" said Anton. "I mean, I'll reschedule. Let me send a text."

"Not from here," said Stephen. "Dead zone, remember? But you can use the phone downstairs if you want."

After dressing in his tee and a pair of Stephen's old track bottoms, Anton went ahead to call Christian. He pulled his mobile phone from his pocket, and sure enough, not a single bar showed on the display. Moreover, he was shocked to see the digital clock showing the time as after five. Where had the afternoon gone? He thumbed through the contact list and found Christian's mobile phone number, then placed his mobile on the hall table, lifted the heavy handset, and still hesitant with the circular dial, rang the number.

"Hello," said a man's voice, harsh and unknown.

"Sorry. Is this Christian Phillips's number?" said Anton, wondering for a second if he'd dialed the wrong number.

"Who's wants to know?" said the voice, a little more aggressive now and possibly a little drunk. He wondered why somebody else would be answering Christian's mobile phone.

"A friend," said Anton. "Is he there? Can you put him on?"

"Is that Anthony?" said the voice he suddenly recognized as that of Max, Christian's new partner. "What do you want?"

"Anton. I need to check something with—" began Anton.

"How many fucking times does he need to tell you to leave us the fuck alone?" shouted the man. "Why don't people like you ever know when to quit? Chris doesn't need your kind of fucked-up—"

"You're right, he doesn't," said Anton, more to himself, calmly replacing the receiver into the cradle. So, he thought, smooth-talking Max in touch with his feelings might not be so cool after all. Well, Christian had made his bed. When he turned around, Stephen stood at the bottom of the stairs, a frown creasing his brow.

"Did you hear any of that?" asked Anton.

"Who's Christian?" asked Stephen.

He thought briefly about telling a white lie, to call him a friend, but Stephen deserved better.

"My ex," said Anton with a sigh. "And that was his new boyfriend, Max, swearing at me down the telephone."

"Are you and Christian still—?" he asked, his face dark.

"No. No!" interrupted Anton, moving over to grasp Stephen's upper arm. "This week he called me, asked to meet up and talk, and I agreed. Stupidly. I don't even know what it's about. And I don't really care now. This is where I want to be."

Anton pulled Stephen's head toward his own and hugged him hard until Stephen's body relaxed and he returned the clasp. As he pulled away, Anton kissed him on the cheek and was relieved to see the doctor smiling again.

"Can I stay the night?" asked Anton sheepishly. "I mean, if I ask nicely?"

"So that I can watch you sleep?" said Stephen.

"Who said anything about sleeping?" said Anton with a smirk.

"Incorrigible," said Stephen, laughing and springing into action. "Go to the kitchen and choose a bottle of red from the wall rack. I'm going to light the fire and make us an early dinner. I hope you're okay with simple pasta."

An hour later and the "simple pasta" turned out to be the best meal Anton had eaten in as long as he could remember. Flat ribbon pappardelle pasta cooked with strips of beef and wild mushrooms together with garlic bread and a side salad of sliced vine tomatoes, set on spinach and basil leaves, drizzled with a delicious vinaigrette dressing. Fortunately he had picked out a good bottle of Italian Chianti from Stephen's impressive collection that nicely complemented the food. Instead of the formality of the dining room or kitchen, Stephen chose to serve the meal on the coffee table in the sitting room.

After eating, Stephen perched himself at one end of the long sofa, his back resting against the arm of the chair, staring at the wineglass twirled between his fingers. Anton got up from the single armchair, which was too near to the fire's heat, and did the same, sitting cross-legged facing Stephen from the other end of the settee.

When Stephen met his eyes, he smiled oddly and shook his head.

"You're like Sebastian in so many ways," he said. "That's where he used to perch. Like a bookend."

Anton nodded but said nothing, reluctant to spoil the mood of intimacy and afraid that talk of Sebastian might darken the doctor's spirits. But Stephen continued on anyway.

"We built this place together. Weekend after weekend building, decorating, or gardening, barely left any time for each other. And then before we'd even finished he became sick."

Again Anton said nothing. If Stephen was ready to talk, he told himself, he would be happy to listen.

"A consequence—a downside perhaps—of being a GP is that we become desensitized to the suffering of the diseased and dying. Not uncaring you understand, but inured. It's part of our calling, to heal, or at least make those who can't be healed as comfortable as possible. But when you deal with death so often, you need to become armor plated. If not, you'd go crazy. And then one day, when one or the other happens to someone close to home, a family member or loved one, there's no armor in the world that can shield you.

"At the time I was so caught up in my work and this house that I was blind to the symptoms. If you'd known Sebastian, you'd have seen what a health freak he was, someone who became unbearable if he had to stay indoors for more than a few hours. But even the healthiest of people develop cancer. A tough one too, because with carcinoma of the esophagus, the symptoms aren't obvious—a common sore throat, a dry cough or trouble swallowing—and usually by the time cancer is detected, it's already at an advanced stage. I thought nothing of his irritable cough when he headed off for summer, almost eight weeks with a specialist travel company. And even on our regular calls he usually sounded fine. But as soon as he returned I could tell something wasn't right and got him straight to a specialist.

"When the hospital ran out of options, including chemotherapy, I brought him home to care for him here. He couldn't understand why I wasn't able to cure him. I could sense it in his eyes, a kind of questioning, pleading every time I checked in on him. After all, wasn't that what I did, make sick people well? But by God he fought like a prizefighter, as tough and stubborn as a mule. And then the day before he died, before I left for my evening appointments and the night nurse arrived to take over, he appeared relaxed, not any better but calm and clearheaded. And I suppose that at some point during the day, he had come to terms with his mortality.

"After we cremated him, I vowed to myself never to get that close to anyone ever again. For the past two years I've managed pretty well. But I'm surrounded by reminders of Sebastian: the cottage, countryside, our friends. Hiding out from the world makes grief fester and even harder to bear. That's why I decided to do something about it."

Africa, thought Anton, but said nothing. Susanna had mentioned his plan to do charity work in the New Year.

"And then you crashed into my life," said Stephen.

"Literally," said Anton, grinning.

"Anton. The moment you walked into the kitchen, I knew I wanted you. Before you even opened your mouth," said Stephen, fondness shining from his eyes. "I didn't want to, because you stirred up old feelings, ones I'd been trying so hard to control. And when you blundered into my room that night and then asked me if I wanted company, I almost crumbled."

"I wish you had. I thought you'd taken an instant dislike to me," said Anton.

"Yes, and I'm sorry," said Stephen, his eyes pleading for forgiveness. "My heavy-handed attempt at self-protection."

"Believe it or not, I understand now. I've spent the past eight months trying to do the same. Anyway, it doesn't matter. I like this. A lot."

"Me too," said Stephen, reaching out and pulling Anton's feet into his lap. While talking, he rubbed his thumbs along the bridge of each foot. "Tell me about you. You had a boyfriend? Christian. How long were you together?"

"Three years," said Anton and couldn't keep the derision from his voice. He gave Stephen an abridged version of the relationship, the good things about Christian as well as the things he disliked, and how in the end Christian had found someone else. Stephen muttered the name Max, remembering the rather unpleasant voice he had overheard on the telephone earlier in the evening. Rather than tell the ugly truth about why he was dumped, Anton told Stephen that Christian wanted different things.

"This is going to sound like a strange question, but did Sebastian smoke?" asked Anton.

"He did, once upon a time in his dim and distant past, before we met. But while I knew him, he wouldn't have dared. Besides, he was an outdoors fanatic and needed his lungs healthy and uncongested," said Stephen, but then gave Anton quizzical look. "Why do you ask?"

Anton thought about telling Stephen about the apparition in the window but then decided to keep things simple.

"I found a packet of Camel cigarettes and an old-fashioned steel lighter. In the drawer of that lovely old desk in the spare room," he said. "I've never noticed you and any of your friends smoking. So I assumed they must have belonged to Sebastian."

"That desk was left by the previous owner. Or the packet could have been left by holiday renters from when my father rented the place out," said Stephen, putting a hand behind his neck and squeezing. "Although to be honest, nobody ever went in that room. It was used— still is—as a storage space. We never quite got around to decorating that one or the end bedroom."

"That's the third time I've noticed you rubbing the back of your neck," said Anton. "Are you okay?"

"Fine. Stiff. Stresses of the job," said Stephen, stifling a yawn.

Anton got up and walked to Stephen's end of the sofa. Stephen watched him curiously but said nothing.

"Move forward," he ordered.

"What for?"

"Do you trust me?"

"Of course I do," said Stephen.

"Then shuffle forward and I'll show you."

Once Stephen had moved forward, he squeezed in behind him and cradled the doctor's head on his chest. With confident strokes, he began massaging the back of Stephen's neck using his thumbs and fingers, eliciting rumbled purring from the doctor.

"My grandmother had an Indian student boarding with us when I was twelve. He taught us a couple of Ayurvedic massage techniques. A great way to relieve stress."

"That does feel amazing. And what did you teach him?" asked Stephen, tilting his head back farther and smirking.

"Actually, I taught him how to sail," said Anton, resting his cheek on the top of Stephen's head. "Toppers on the Gannel Estuary in Newquay. The principles of sailing are the same even for larger sailboats. Maybe I can teach you one day? When the weather gets warmer?"

Stephen fell silent then, and Anton wondered for a moment what he had said.

"We'll see."

By ten o'clock, after Stephen had apologized for yawning a few times, Anton suggested they go to bed. Together they went through Stephen's nightly routine of switching off lights and checking windows and doors to ensure they were bolted. Once they reached the bedroom, Anton excused himself to use the bathroom while Stephen undressed and got into bed, leaving just the bedside lamp burning.

When Anton eventually emerged, Stephen had climbed into the far side of the bed, his head toward Anton, but appeared to be asleep. Anton undressed quietly and completely, pulled back the covers, and lay down naked facing him. Sleep made Stephen's features even more handsome, relaxed and boyish. Even though he ached to touch the man, he decided not to disturb his hard-won sleep and switched off the bedside lamp.

As Anton finally felt himself giving in to sleep, he heard Stephen's whispered voice in his ear.

"Turn over."

Anton opened his eyes to see Stephen's face hovering over him. He did as asked and rolled onto his side, his back to Stephen. Immediately Stephen's warm body encased him, an arm placed beneath his neck, the other folded around Anton's chest.

"Even if I can't sleep much, at least I can enjoy this," he said before kissing Anton on the back of the neck.

CHAPTER 10
WEEKEND

ANTON WOKE Sunday morning with Stephen still asleep, wrapped around him, his face pressed into Anton's neck. Clicks and groans from the radiator beneath the window indicated a heating system that had already woken. While the exposed side of Anton's face still felt the pinch of overnight chill, from the neck down, beneath the plump white duvet, he lay bathed in their combined body heat, a feeling he wanted to savor for as long as possible. Pressed into the crevice between his upper thighs he could feel the hot strain of Stephen's morning erection. He would have to move eventually, traitorous bodily functions already demanding attention. For a couple of moments more, though, he remained still and mulled over the implausibility of the past day.

All thoughts of Christian had evaporated. Apart from the intense physical connection with Stephen, better than anything Anton had ever experienced—practiced, sensual, and mutually satisfying—he found the doctor's company effortless and agreeable, as though they had known each other all their lives. Waking now in the knowledge of their simple act of sleeping together through the night made Anton's heart overflow with affection. Even if the new morning brought about a change in the man, a distance, a need for detachment and privacy, he would value their shared afternoon and night together for the rest of his life.

Signs of a winter's morning pierced the room—bleached winter sunlight bleeding in from beneath the edge of the curtain and the excited chirp of birds beyond the window. Gently lifting Stephen's arm from around him, he slipped away to the side of the bed, then pulled his warm pillow down and laid Stephen's arm on top without waking him, smoothing the duvet back into place.

Pulling on the shorts and tee Stephen had lent him, he crept down to the kitchen and used the tiny bathroom at the back. Afterward he set about finding the right equipment for tea making. Opening cupboards and drawers at random, he enjoyed exploring the doctor's kitchen, finding out what type of drinks and foods he stocked, what kind of kitchen products he preferred to buy. By the time he had boiled the kettle and made tea for them both, he found himself absently humming. Standing still for a moment, he shook his head and warned himself to be cautious. Early days, he thought, and in Stephen's mind this might have only been a comforting diversion.

When he returned to the bedroom carrying two mugs of hot tea, Stephen had already pulled himself into a sitting position on the bed.

"What time is it?" he said, yawning.

"Almost eight," said Anton, placing the tea mugs on the bedside cabinet next to Stephen and then moving across to pull open the bedroom curtains. "You've been in the land of nod for ten hours."

"You're not serious!" said Stephen, reaching for his wristwatch on the side of the bed. He stared incredulous at the display. "Last time I slept that long I must have been a teenager."

Anton laughed. With his haystack of blond hair in disarray and sleep-fuddled expression, Anton could almost imagine the man as a teenager. He sat down on the side of the bed, not too close, his insecurities rising again, unsure whether intimacy would be the norm in the cold light of morning.

"I enjoyed yesterday. Very much," he said, his hands planted on the mattress either side of him, turning to Stephen before dropping his gaze to the quilt. "More than I've enjoyed anything in as long as I can remember."

Before Anton realized what was happening, Stephen had reached out, pulled him backward down onto the bed, and planted his lips firmly onto Anton's. At once relieved and aroused, he kissed back until Stephen pulled away.

"Does that mean you're staying?" he asked, gazing into Anton's eyes, his hand slipping beneath the front of Anton's tee and gently brushing his chest and nipples. "Because there's a whole lot more where that came from. And I don't know about you, but my engine's already running."

"Later, tiger," laughed Anton, pushing away and giving Stephen's stiff cock a tweak. "Right now I need to get some fresh air. Couple of miles run at least. And as I don't have a clue where to go, I'll need a local guide with me so I don't get lost. After that we can have a long hot shower together, followed by a day of whatever else you and your supercharged engine desire. And then I'll drive back tonight. Deal?"

"Deal. Give me fifteen minutes," said Stephen, reaching for the tea.

"I'll give you ten," said Anton, tossing Stephen's shorts at his head and turning toward the bedroom door. "And I'll meet you out front."

"Anton," called Stephen.

Anton stopped and turned to see the doctor grinning fondly at him.

"First of all, thank you. For staying over. I like having you here."

"Good. Because I like being here," said Anton, the side of his head resting against the doorframe. "And?"

"Best not leave the house like that," replied Stephen, nodding toward the significant bulge in Anton's shorts. "You never know who might be walking their dog."

Out in the crisp fresh air, Stephen led them at a solid pace back down the lane where Anton's car had crashed. He slowed to point out the spot, one that Anton had not seen since climbing free from the wreckage a month before. A shudder went through him when Stephen pointed out the long white scar running along the base of the granite wall. Once past the scene, Stephen led the way onto the open moor along narrow dirt tracks, many waterlogged, which required careful maneuvering by the doctor. A couple of times Anton huffed when their pace slowed due to Stephen's insistence on picking out a safe route around the puddles. When they reached a stretch of tarmac, Anton burst into a sprint and hurtled past Stephen with a flourish but came to a sudden halt when he glanced back to see Stephen climbing over a stile hidden in the hedgerow.

For most of the hour's run, the weather behaved well, despite the appearance of heavy rainclouds, but as they pounded along a country lane, their luck ran out and the heavens finally opened. By the time they had bolted into an old wooden bus shelter, both were soaked through. Despite being sodden, nothing could dampen Anton's spirits. After flinging himself down on the bench, he shook the water from his hair like a shaggy dog after a swim in the sea.

"Once this lets up a little, we ought to head back," said Stephen, standing at the entrance, hands on hips, trying to survey the deluge. All along the mouth of the shelter's roof, water cascaded like a curtain, obscuring much of the road beyond.

"Until then," said Anton, reaching out and pulling at the band of Stephen's shorts. "Let's think of ways to keep ourselves amused."

"Insatiable," said Stephen but allowed himself to be pulled down onto the bench. With his fingertips, Anton traced the muscles beneath the damp sports shirt, around the pectoral, and over the nipple before putting his hand at the back of the doctor's neck and pulling his mouth down onto his own. Hot and moist, their tongues wrestled, and before long Anton felt the tug of arousal in his shorts. When he finally pulled his head away, he let the fingers of his right hand trace the scar down Stephen's face.

"How did this happen?"

"Looks sinister, doesn't it?"

"Sinister, no. Sexy as hell, yes."

The comment brought an almost shy grin to the doctor's face that made Anton's heart tug.

"I was six years old. Bicycle accident on my grandfather's allotment. Stupid. Fell into barbed wire fencing. Lucky I didn't lose the eye, actually. But it was the best thing that ever happened to me."

"How so?"

"Twenty stitches, four days in hospital, and then back for regular checkups over the next three months. After that I knew."

Anton smiled. "That you wanted to be a doctor?"

"Exactly. Not one of those childhood whims about being a fireman one day and a pilot the next. I knew. Not a lot of six-year-olds can tell you that. I've known people fresh from university with good degrees who still have no idea what they want to do."

Anton leaned forward and kissed the scar. "Sometimes good things come from bad."

"That's one way of looking at it."

"So is that you, Stephen?" said Anton, noticing that the clatter of rainfall had subsided to a constant but light dripping. "The kind of person who makes up his mind what he wants and sticks to it?"

Stephen answered with a sly grin and by pulling Anton in for another embrace. Even wet through, or perhaps especially so, the doctor's body felt incredible, lean but muscled. Without releasing the kiss, Stephen pulled Anton onto his lap, face to face, their erections pressing into each other, the doctor's hands cupped firmly beneath Anton's cheeks.

"Do you mind that I want this so much?" said Stephen, brushing the middle finger of one hand into the crack of Anton's backside.

"Absolutely not," said Anton, his hand slipping beneath the band of Stephen's underpants and stroking the doctor's molten erection. "Because I want this just as much."

"Not here, though, Anton," said Stephen, pulling away and resting their foreheads together. "Sorry, but I need to maintain some level of respectability with the neighbors."

"So you don't want any little old ladies having a show while they're waiting for a bus? Spoilsport."

"Don't think it would go down too well with the local church group," said Stephen, grinning and sucking Anton's bottom lip, just as the phone in his shorts pocket sounded.

Anton had brought his own mobile phone with him, Stephen providing them both with waterproof bags, knowing they might reach a spot with a good connection. Even though he wanted to be exactly where he was, he also felt the need to call Christian. After climbing off Stephen's lap, he watched the doctor walk outside into the clearing day to take his call. First of all he thought about calling Christian directly to apologize for missing him. But fearing Max might pick up again, he decided to call Julie instead. After a few pleasantries, he got down to business.

"The reason I'm calling is because I need a favor."

"Go on."

"Could you pass on a message to Christian for me?"

"Oh yes?" she replied tentatively.

"No, no. It's nothing like that. I was supposed to meet up with him in town yesterday evening. I think he was passing me some post or something. He didn't exactly say. But I had another commitment. I tried to call and let him know, but Max answered his phone. So I've no idea if he got the message or not."

"For Christ's sake," huffed Julie, immediately irritated. "Has Max done that to you too? It's like he's vetting Christian's calls."

"And I guess he's more polite to you than he was to me."

"Oh, Anton. You poor thing. Don't worry. I'll pass the message on somehow. Now, is it me, or do you sound really happy?"

"I am," said Anton and could not help smiling to himself. "I'm doing really well."

"I can tell," said Julie, intrigued. "Anything you want to tell me?"

"Not yet, Julie. Don't want to jinx things. But I am good," he said and meant it. "Got to go. Say hi to Paul for me."

Stephen strolled back in, his carnal attention focused solely on Anton, which sent blood pounding back into Anton's subsiding erection. On noticing Anton putting his phone away, his smile slipped for a second.

"My friend Julie. To let her know where I am and why I'm happy not to be home right now. Don't worry, no details given."

Stephen's grin widened. He came forward and pulled the seated Anton into a fierce embrace, his head resting on the doctor's chest.

"How about you?" asked Anton, feeling the rumble of his voice in Stephen's stomach.

"That was Martin. They're in London next weekend for an antiques fair. Want to know if I fancied joining them."

"And?"

"I don't know," said Stephen. "Not keen on tagging along while they trawl through old furniture, but it would be nice to get away for a weekend. They usually end up booking dinner at a recently rave-reviewed restaurant. Just not a big fan of staying in hotels."

The words were out of Anton's mouth before he had a chance to think.

"Then don't. Come and stay with me."

"Really?" said Stephen, pulling Anton's chin up to look him full in the face. "Look, I wasn't fishing. I don't want to put you out."

"You won't. I'd be honored to have you stay. And if you want, I can be your date for dinner."

Together with a gentle shake of his head, the smile Stephen gave him melted his heart.

"You're too much. And I'd like that. Very much."

"Me too," said Anton, peering mischievously up at Stephen. "If only to see the look on Gallagher's face."

"Right, come on," said Stephen, laughing and pulling Anton up. "Another few miles, a hot shower, and then I'm going to take you to lunch. I've just thought of the perfect place."

Once again Stephen led the way but this time mainly off road. Helped by the past downpour and rainfall over the past month, sections of the pathways had become waterlogged and difficult to negotiate, although Stephen became a master of picking a way around. This meant, of course, that Anton had to slow down, wait, and cautiously follow the doctor until they reached a dry spot of pathway, which became more and more frustrating. When they reached another puddle, this one almost a small lake, Anton's patience gave out.

"This way looks easier."

"No, trust me, Anton, this way is better. The sloped edges that side are deceptively slippery."

"Not if you—"

"Watch out!"

But the warning came too late, and as Anton's left foot slipped away, the right one came with it, and he ended up in the chill and gritty water of the mud pool. Submerged briefly, he sat up and, through the dirty rivulets running down his face, saw Stephen crouched at the edge. For a second he wondered if the doctor was having an attack of some kind, his hands clutched across his chest, his head tucked into his body. Beginning to stand, Anton's foot slipped again, and instead he found himself splashing onto his knees in the brown sludge. This time when looking over, he realized the spasms Stephen was experiencing were in fact fits of laughter.

"Thank you very much," said Anton, indignant, hands on hips.

But Stephen couldn't speak,

"Hey, doctor duck," said Anton, trying to stand again and now laughing himself. "A little help here."

"I'm sorry," said Stephen, unfolding and stretching a hand out to assist.

Anton was tempted to pull the doctor in with him but decided he wanted out of the ice-cold sludge.

"Poor baby," chuckled Stephen, pulling Anton into a hug and in the process getting covered with muddy water. No matter that Anton tried to pull away to minimize the wetness. Stephen kept him close, almost relishing their shared dampness.

Despite the cold of the day, they walked back the rest of the way, this time carefully avoiding puddles. Only as Anton stood outside the front door of the coach house, while Stephen closed the front gate, did he look down and assess himself.

"Stephen, I can't traipse mud through the house."

"You're not going to. Follow me."

Stephen led the way along a small path to the back of the cottage. Two bamboo partitions stood out from the back wall next to where Anton thought the downstairs toilet must be housed. Beneath the partitions was simple square decking set on a mound of stones. Stephen stopped, reached in, and the next thing the sound of running water filled the air. Before long thick, white steam crept out from all around and in between the bamboo.

"You have an outdoor shower?"

"Sebastian's idea. He wanted to be able to clean off before coming into the house. But he only used it during the summer months. Come on. You look like you could do with warming up."

As soon as Anton stood beneath the hot water, he felt incredible, refreshed and cocooned. Fully clothed still, he closed his eyes, turned his head up into the revitalizing spray, and let the bulk of the grit be rinsed from his face. After a few moments, he sensed rather than heard Stephen behind him. Without a word, the doctor began tugging at the waist of Anton's shirt, getting him to raise his arms and pull the shirt over his head. Once his shorts had been yanked off and discarded, Stephen came up behind him naked and wrapped his hands around Anton's chest. They stayed that way for a long time, swaying gently while the water cleansed them, both men's arousals growing.

"Shame I don't have any condoms out here," Stephen whispered into Anton's ear.

"Maybe just as well. I've still got grains of dirt in rather awkward places."

"Then let me help you get cleaned up first."

Only as Stephen used the soap, shampoo, and the small sponge left there did the thought that this was all Sebastian's cross his mind. Not that he cared. Even though he had never met the man, the more he knew about him, the more he approved. Liked his choices. A shower in the back garden was something Anton had always wanted. But such a thing would be neither practical nor private in suburban Newquay, with neighbors peering into each other's gardens.

A gasp brought him out of his reverie as Stephen's soap-coated finger penetrated him, cleansed him, and then invaded once more. Anton tilted his head back onto Stephen's shoulder and murmured.

"Are you sure you don't have any?"

"Yes. And before you ask, I'm not letting you go now to go fetch them. Let's try something else instead."

Both lathered up and with Stephen still behind Anton, the doctor pushed his erection between Anton's upper thighs. At the same time he reached in front and grasped Anton's shaft. With the push and pull of the doctor's hips, Anton loved the feel of the hot cock sliding between his thighs and nudging his ball sac. Once again Stephen grabbed Anton's chin and pulled him around for a deep, passionate kiss. While their bodies danced together this way, Stephen's practiced hand brought him closer and closer until a moan formed within their kiss. Almost at the same time, Stephen's pumping action became erratic, cannonballing hard into Anton. With a shared groan of pleasure, they sprayed their joint come into the falling water.

Sebastian had thought of everything, and a tall cupboard just inside the back door housed piles of plump white towels. Stephen handed one to Anton, and they toweled off back in the warmth of the kitchen. While drying Anton's back, Stephen threw out suggestions for lunch.

"Okay. We have two choices. There's a small airfield about an hour and a half's drive away with a restaurant that overlooks the runway. The Airman or Pilot, I think it's called, but apparently they do a very nice brunch. And while we eat, we can sit and watch light airplanes taking off and landing. Quite spectacular, and recommended—of course—by Martin and Gallagher."

With his head turned away, Anton toweled his hair dry and was grateful Stephen didn't see his smile slip. Anywhere near airplanes and he would not be able to eat a scrap, would be lucky to hold down conversation, let alone any food.

"Or?"

"Chez Stephen. A decent but little known rural kitchen not far from Hawk's Tor and run by a rather dishy general practitioner. He serves up a somewhat simpler affair of eggs hollandaise with freshly brewed coffee followed by apricot pancakes and clotted cream."

"Did you just call yourself dishy?"

"And what would you call me?" said Stephen, dropping his towel into the laundry basket.

"Dishy doesn't even begin to describe you," said Anton, leering at the doctor, who stood deliciously naked.

"So before we both decide what to wear, what do you want to do?"

"I think I like the idea of the rural kitchen. And spending more time with the dishy doctor."

"Good. In which case let's wear sweats again. Help yourself from my wardrobe upstairs while I start to fix lunch."

"A naked chef?"

"Don't be ridiculous. I'm going to be wearing an apron."

That afternoon, after a satisfying array of food, they sat back on the sofa, talked, snoozed, and woke, before making love again in front of the dying embers of the log fire. At around four, Anton reluctantly announced his departure. Progressively through the afternoon the air outside had become chillier, and Anton worried about driving back on slippery roads. After he made sure Stephen had his home address, they parted at the front gate, both promising to keep in touch every day, both looking forward to the weekend to come.

About to get in his car, Stephen called to Anton and came trotting over. For a second Anton wondered if he had left something behind as he had done the time before. Instead Stephen quickly surveyed the deserted lane before grasping hold of Anton and pulling him into a fierce embrace. When he pulled away, and a bemused Anton looked into Stephen's sparkling eyes, the doctor said simply, "One for the road."

CHAPTER 11
LONDON

"So this is home. Nice. Not quite what I expected," said Stephen, striding over the threshold, his gaze scouring Anton's living room and landing on the three sealed boxes against the sitting room wall, items that had become invisible to Anton. "When did you move in?"

"They're full of books," said Anton, closing the door and coming to stand next to him. Nervous at having Stephen to visit, his heart had hammered with a mixture of anxiousness and anticipation on seeing the Range Rover pull up outside his block. Even more so when he saw Stephen decked out against the chill November day in black jeans, black polo neck sweater, and ash jacket. That casual look, together with his blond thatch, made him even hotter as he strolled confidently toward the block of flats. All morning, while he busied himself preparing for the visit, Anton had begun to realize the inadequacies of his private sanctuary. "I'm still trying to find the right bookcase. A work in progress."

"Call Martin. He'll do you a good deal," said Stephen with a simple shrug before indicating the small travel case he had brought with him. "Where should I drop this?"

In contrast to Anton's discomfort, Stephen seemed completely at ease. Perhaps his vocation had afforded him sufficient house calls that, unlike Anton, he no longer felt any concern when stepping into another person's private space.

"In the bedroom on the right," said Anton, indicating the one bedroom along the small hallway. "The bathroom's opposite. No en suites here, I'm afraid."

Without hesitation, Stephen headed to the doorway and stepped inside. Anton trailed behind and found Stephen examining the space, his bag already placed on the room's one small chair. Everything had been freshly cleaned, vacuumed and polished, and a new navy duvet covered the bed. Anton had even placed white and gold cushions from the living room in front of the matching navy pillows to try to make the place appear more stylish.

"One bedroom apartment," said Anton anxiously, noticing Stephen's gaze coming to rest on the double. "Bed's a fair bit smaller than yours. I can always sleep on the sofa—"

"Anton," said Stephen, twisting around and gathering him into an embrace. "Stop apologizing. It's fine. And I'm here to see you, in case you'd forgotten."

"Sorry. I'm nervous," he replied.

"About what?" said Stephen, sounding genuinely surprised. He tightened his hug until Anton finally felt his body relaxing.

"I don't know. You're in my world, I suppose. And I want you to like it as much as I do."

"Give me a chance. I've just arrived," said Stephen, pecking him on the cheek and releasing him. "Go make some coffee and I'll have a nose around."

Anton busied himself in the kitchen, making freshly ground coffee using the percolator he had not used since moving in. Within minutes the kitchen filled with the aromatic smell, which also brought Stephen. While Anton pulled mugs down from a kitchen cupboard, Stephen crossed the room, placed his chin on Anton's shoulder, and wrapped his arms around his waist.

"Mm. Smells almost as good as you," said Stephen, rubbing his stubble into the soft skin beneath Anton's ear and kissing him on the lobe.

Anton loved feeling Stephen's hard body pressing against his back and felt himself becoming aroused.

"Hope you don't mind, but I closed the curtains in the bedroom. Wondered if we could find something to keep ourselves occupied while coffee's brewing."

Anton twisted around to face him, put his arms around his neck, and kissed him. Stephen returned the embrace hungrily and pushed his hips into Anton's, their erections rubbing against each other. While still exploring each other's mouths, Stephen started to unbutton Anton's shirt and then slipped his hands inside to feel the rise and fall of his chest and stomach.

"Coffee can wait," said Anton, leading the way into the bedroom.

Despite the sudden rush of passion, sex between them was unhurried. Since their encounter a week before, they had texted three times each day and phoned at least once. After more than one of their late-night calls, Anton had needed to relieve his arousal. Although he hadn't asked, he felt sure Stephen had done the same.

Having the man in his bed now, he wanted to try out all the carnal imaginings his mind had conjured over the past week. Seven days was too long to be apart, he complained to himself, when any other couple would have been trying something new every day at this stage of their relationship. But his mind also conceded the practicalities that kept them apart.

Wrapped tightly together now, they tasted each other's bodies and sought out small things to turn each other on, fingers trailing up and down each other's back, thighs, and backsides, stopping to press or squeeze gently as they kissed passionately. Anton's yelp of surprise that quickly turned to moans of pleasure when Stephen's tongue probed deep inside him; Stephen gasping with elation when Anton pushed him onto his back and rode him like a Grand National jockey. Both watched the other's face for triggers, a moment of rapture, selflessly wanting to give the other pleasure and store the knowledge for future lovemaking. Even as Stephen filled him, pounding his sweet spot and sending waves of joyous current rippling through him, the doctor added more sensations, overloading his senses—pulling him in to kiss deeply, leaning up and sucking and biting on a nipple until Anton's body erupted, unable to take any more. When the final moan escaped his lips, Anton felt sure the sound came from elsewhere until his ejaculation reached Stephen's chest and face, which had Stephen climaxing almost simultaneously in a sweaty heap.

"Don't know about you," said Stephen as they helped each other clean up. "But I've been looking forward to that all week."

"Double ditto," said Anton, stopping to collect a kiss from Stephen before pulling his head back and gazing deep into the doctor's eyes. "And did I mention you're incredible?"

"Am I?" asked Stephen softly, one eyebrow lifting.

"And if there's anything, you know, that you want to do," said Anton, turning to rearrange his pillow. "In bed, I mean. Just want you to know, it's fine by me."

"Nice to know. But just so *you* know, what we just did is more than enough."

Stephen lowered himself down onto his back and tucked his hands behind his head on the pillows, scanning Anton's face.

"No, I just wanted to say," continued Anton, a frown flickering across his face, still not meeting the doctor's eyes, "that I'm okay with whatever you want."

"Whatever *we* want, you mean. I would never do anything we didn't both agree…," began Stephen. "Anton?"

"Yes," said Anton, finally meeting Stephen's concerned gaze.

"Is this about Christian?"

Despite the sudden dryness of his throat and the sting in his eyes, he held Stephen's stare.

"He said I wasn't enough. And I want to be enough for you."

"*Uninspiring and unadventurous both in and out of the sack*" had been Christian's exact words when Anton had commented one night after a more rough than usual sex session. Red welts had been left on the back of Anton's neck where Christian had thrust his head down into the pillow. As Christian climaxed on top of him, Anton had barely had enough room or leverage to breathe.

"Then he's even more of an idiot than I thought. You're amazing, Anton."

This time Stephen pulled Anton down on top of him into an embrace, their chests pressed together until Anton shared the regular thump of Stephen's heart through his own rib cage. The realization washed over Anton like a spring tide. Stephen and he made love. With Christian he had only experienced sex. Eventually Anton rolled off Stephen, and they settled down on the bed with the doctor's head cradled on Anton's shoulder, his chest rising and falling, his mussed-up hair occasionally brushing and tickling Anton beneath the chin. They lay together unspeaking, enjoying the simple pleasure of each other's presence.

"How's the neck?" asked Anton, breaking the silence.

"Been fine all week, thanks to your magic hands. But another massage would be very welcome. I'm also sleeping better. Especially after our nightly calls."

Another lull fell, comfortable and familiar, Anton cocooned by the warmth of the doctor's body up against him.

"Hey, let's play five things," said Anton eventually, while trailing his fingers through Stephen's hair.

"What's that?"

"Five important things we ought to know about each other. That few other people in the world would know. You start. Five things."

"Such as?"

"Anything. Things you really like."

"I really like you," said Stephen, leaning in and kissing Anton on the nipple.

"Come on! Martin and Gallagher figured that one out long before we did. No, five things other people won't know. Okay, I'll go first," said Anton, and he noticed how Stephen listened patiently while smiling at the ceiling. "I like the trailers before a film. You know, like at the cinema or on a DVD, those little teasers of things to come. A lot of people find them irritating and, on DVD anyway, skip them. But not me. I love them. Two, I like people to be honest rather than telling white lies to spare another person's feelings. And I guess that goes hand in hand with the fact that I hate surprises, especially bad ones. I've had my share of those. Three, I am a huge fan of foreplay. A lot of men prefer to head straight for the main event, but sorry, I am not one of them. Time should stand still in the bedroom."

"Interesting. And how am I doing so far?" said Stephen.

"You have reached platinum star status," said Anton, hugging Stephen's head into his body. "Four, I love kids and want to have them one day. Adopted, I think. Because I'd like to believe I was giving a life a second chance."

When he looked down at Stephen, the doctor was still smiling thoughtfully into space. On hearing the rustle of Anton's head turning on the pillow, his gaze swung around.

"And?"

"And what?"

"You said five things. What's the fifth?"

Anton became anxious then. He hated to show weakness to anyone and let out a small sigh before continuing.

"I'm a chronic aerophobic. I have an abject fear of flying and everything related. Even the thought of being near a plane makes me break out in a cold sweat and want to rush for the nearest toilet bowl. I know that sounds pathetic, but back in the eighties my mother and father died in a plane crash on their way to attend a wedding in Ireland. It was all over the news. The plane needed to make an emergency landing and crashed before they reached the runway. Out of a hundred and thirty passengers, fifty-five died, my parents among them."

Although Stephen said nothing, he muttered an expletive and squeezed Anton's thigh in sympathy. When Anton looked down at him, the whimsical smile on the doctor's face had slipped, and he stared ahead, deep in thought. Almost instantly Anton regretted ever having started his pathetic five things game. Now he worried about the thoughts racing through the doctor's mind, if he disliked weakness in others, and whether this admission had diluted Anton's appeal. In part, Anton could understand the sentiment—if he suffered from an abject fear of something so trivial, what other hang-ups and phobias could he be hiding? Hadn't Christian stated the same thing about him? That his fear had put limits on their relationship. But he had really warmed to Stephen and wanted the doctor to value him as an equal.

Onto the fragile canvas of every blossoming relationship, there comes a point when the hand of one lover dabs the first imperfection. Sometimes this flaw enhances the portrait. At other times the image is irrevocably damaged, the fatal imperfection.

"We're meeting everyone at the restaurant at seven thirty," said Stephen eventually, after a few worrying moments had passed. He let his fingertips drift down Anton's inner thigh.

"Everyone?"

"Sean and Federico are in town too," he said, tilting his head to glance up at Anton. "Hope that's okay."

"Do they know you're bringing someone?"

"Of course. Martin had to make reservations."

"And do they know the someone you're bringing is me?"

"No," he said with a mischievous grin and a sparkle in his eyes. "Despite getting grilled. I told him it's someone I recently bumped into at the hospital."

"Which is not strictly a lie. Do you want to take a shower?"

"What time is it now?"

"Three thirty."

"Plenty of time, then."

Stephen's hand trailed back up Anton's leg and gently squeezed his balls. Anton hadn't realized he'd been holding his breath until then, but this intimate gesture finally broke the spell, and his body relaxed with relief.

"You are insatiable. What about coffee, doctor duck?" he said, placing his hand over the doctor's but making no attempt to move it away. Instead he pulled Stephen's face up to meet his own and kissed him.

"Mm. Coffee's not going anywhere."

Eventually Anton managed to prize them out of the bedroom, even though Stephen insisted on them both staying in their underwear. He lounged comfortably on the black leather sofa like a male model from an underwear catalogue while Anton made a fresh pot of coffee and then brought a tray with the coffeepot, two mugs, a carton of milk, and the sugar bowl. He'd tried to find his milk jug but eventually gave up.

"So what do you think of the place?" asked Anton, giving Stephen his coffee and suddenly feeling anxious again. "And don't spare my feelings. You know I'll trust your judgment."

Stephen's gaze measured Anton for a moment before he placed the mug onto a coaster on the smoked glass table and gave Anton his full attention.

"For someone so immersed in art and photography, who can recite artists and their works by heart and even has a not insignificant talent of his own," said Stephen, rescanning the room, "I'm surprised to see bare walls and empty shelves."

"What do you mean?" said Anton.

"Well…. There's not much of *you* in the apartment," said Stephen. "Hospital wards have more personality."

Anton thumped himself down on the sofa next to Stephen. When he scanned the room with fresh eyes, he realized the truth in the doctor's words. Not only had he never put any effort into making the place his own, he had never completely moved in. Most of the furniture had been left by the previous owner. He had abandoned his prized reproductions, photos, and all the furnishings Christian and he had bought together back in the house they once shared. And his conviction that in this newly purchased apartment he had created a sanctuary for himself was nothing short of a lie. He had built a fortress, a prison, a padded cell.

"Shit," he said finally. "You're right. Do you know something else? I've lived here for six months, and you're my first visitor."

"I'm honored," said Stephen, pushing his arm along the back of the sofa and hugging Anton's head to him.

"No," said Anton, gently pushing away. "What I mean is I've never even considered having a housewarming party. Or inviting my sister or any of my neighbors or close friends over. What's wrong with me?"

"Perhaps you're still mourning," said Stephen with a shrug. "For a life you once shared with Christian."

And there it was, plain as daylight. Within a few hours of arriving at Anton's house, Stephen had managed to get to the root of Anton's self-imposed stasis. He had not moved in because he had not moved on. Deep down he treated this place as a halfway house while waiting for a call from Christian, pleading with him to get back together and return to their love nest. Waiting for a call that would never come.

"Thank you for the diagnosis, doctor," said Anton, kissing him on the cheek. "Don't suppose you have a remedy to hand?"

"Simple. What about those things from your grandmother's house? Didn't you say you kept some of your old paintings, photos and things? Let's do a spot of decorating."

"Now?"

"Why not?"

"I couldn't ask you to do that."

"Nonsense," said Stephen, springing up from the sofa. "I'll enjoy myself. Who do you think put up the pictures in my place? And besides, I'm already thinking of ways you can pay me back later."

"I told you. You can have anything you want."

"*We* want. In which case, go and fetch your toolbox."

"Uh—I'm sorry?" said Anton, concern on his face.

"To hang the pictures," said Stephen quizzically, until the penny dropped and they burst into laughter together.

Both still in underwear, they spent the next two hours bringing the apartment to life. They emptied out the two large boxes and retrieved pictures Anton had hidden away in his bedroom closet, deciding where best to put things, dusting them off before arranging them in place. Stephen, it transpired, had a keen eye for where and how best to hang pictures. They worked together so well that Anton barely noticed time slipping by. While Stephen busied himself hammering a nail in the wall, Anton went to make a phone call before heading to the kitchen. Only as he returned carrying two glasses of water did the transformation hit him. The living room still had the modern touch of a new apartment, but now familiar faces and moody watercolors jumped out from the walls or from his solitary cabinet. Above the table Stephen had fixed one of his more challenging works, one his sister had admired, of a lonely Newquay seascape. As he placed the drinks onto the table, he spotted Stephen emptying out the boxes of books and arranging them on the two window ledges, stopping every once in a while to flick through one or the other.

"How could you let these gather dust?" asked Stephen without turning around. "They're amazing."

"I know. And I've had them for years. I can't believe how different everything looks already. Thanks for waking both me and the place up."

"My pleasure. Who were you talking to?" asked Stephen.

"Taxi company. Ordering us a cab for six forty-five."

"I said I'd drive."

"But then you can't drink. And you deserve to relax and have a good time tonight. Anyway, if you drove we'd have to leave early to find somewhere to park. Taking a cab will buy us some time."

"For what?" said Stephen, finally turning around, his eyes filled with mischief.

"Stephen, it's just gone six. No idea where the afternoon went, but we need to get dressed. And we haven't even showered yet."

"Could save some time if we showered together."

"Great minds think alike."

By the time they had finished—a more tricky operation in the restricted space of Anton's combined bath and shower—they had to hurry to change. Stephen was still drying his hair when the taxi driver phoned to let them know he had arrived and was waiting outside. Although getting to the outskirts of Wimbledon proved easy enough, they spent some time navigating the one-way system in busy Saturday evening traffic. By the time they crested the top of Wimbledon Hill, they were already ten minutes late. Nevertheless, Stephen insisted the driver drop them at an ATM machine on the mini roundabout at the beginning of the High Street. After he had finished, the two of them bounced shoulder to shoulder along the pavement, so engrossed in each other's chatter and presence that Anton barely acknowledged the lone figure that peeled away from a small crowd and stood in the middle of the pavement waiting for them.

"Swann?" called the gritty voice, bringing Anton out of his trance.

They came to an abrupt halt before Max, who stood there as rough and solid as ever, sporting the same sneer of a smile he had worn at the gallery opening. Anton wondered why Max was so far from their home in Wandsworth until he remembered the mainline station down the hill and the train line that passed through Wandsworth Common.

"How are you, Max?" said Anton blandly, because he could think of nothing else to say. Even though Max stood his ground well, the beetroot cheeks and watery eyes gave Anton the impression that he had been drinking heavily.

"We're good, aren't we? Chris is home cooking for a dinner party. Got some of your old friends coming round tonight, haven't we?"

Anton recalled how Max often turned statements into a question. And the dig about Christian having a dinner party for their old friends was not lost on him. But he could only imagine Christian's face when Max turned up in his drunken state. Good luck with that, *Chris*, his inner voice quipped.

"Max, this is Stephen," said Anton, remembering the man by his side, who Max had already eyed warily a couple of times.

"Not your new boyfriend, is he?" said Max, and by the smirk on his face he meant the comment as a joke.

Anton turned to look at Stephen then. They had not defined their relationship, and Anton wondered whether Stephen was ready to do so yet. But before he had a chance to say anything, Stephen answered for him.

"Yes, I am," said Stephen, putting his hand into Anton's.

Despite the warm feeling the simple response gave him, Anton couldn't help notice the small crinkle of disapproval between Stephen's eyebrows as he studied Max. No doubt they would have words about this encounter later. For his part, Max squinted curiously back at Stephen, gave him the full once-over before returning his attention to Anton.

"Getting around a bit, aren't you? What happened to the Irish bloke from the painting place?"

"Sean? He's a friend. A good one. Helping a friend in need," said Anton and felt more than a little irritated when Max's attention drifted back to Stephen. "We're meeting him and his partner now. In fact we should be going. We're running late."

"Max. Come on, geezer," called a voice from the small group that had stopped at the corner of the road to wait for him.

"I know you from somewhere, don't I?" said Max directly to Stephen, the voice rumbling with a menacing undercurrent.

"Not much chance of that," said Anton before Stephen could speak. "Stephen's family comes from Devon."

"His face rings a bell, though. Did you used to go to the Dugout in Clapham?"

"Clearly you have me mixed up with somebody else," said Stephen, whose voice had lost all of its previous warmth.

"For fuck's sake, Max," shouted the same voice again. "Move your arse, will you? We need to catch the half past."

"Hang on," said Max, pulling something from his jacket. "Let me have a quick shot of the two of you together. Something to show to Chris. He'll be pleased to see you've finally moved on."

Before either of them had a chance to object, Max had snapped the picture on his phone. Probably not the best of photos either, with both of them looking bemused. Straight afterward, Max trotted away without another word, leaving Stephen and Anton standing there.

"That's your ex's new boyfriend?" asked Stephen once they had resumed their pace.

"Uh-huh."

"So different from you."

"I think that's the point. I guess Christian wanted someone straightforward, more down to earth."

"A thug, you mean."

Anton grinned at the dark sky and linked his arm in Stephen's.

Krystos Taverna sat at the far end of the high street, near to Wimbledon Common. Double-fronted bay windows of clear glass allowed passersby to look into the chaotic heart of the place. Busy already, small parties of between four and six persons were installed in the window seats. Stephen didn't hesitate but pushed open the front door and strode inside. A waiter informed them that Martin had booked a table for twelve in a private dining area at the back of the restaurant and led the way. As soon as Stephen entered and pulled

Anton in after him, a cheer went up. Places had been left vacant for Stephen and his guest at the far end of the table. But everyone else was there, including Stephen's sister, Susie, and her husband, Bob, with two of their friends. Two other unfamiliar faces turned out to be antique shop owners and friends of Martin and Gallagher. Anton hugged each of the already familiar men, laughing as Sean handed Federico a twenty-pound note for a bet he'd clearly lost. Martin put his camera down to hug Anton fiercely, but when he glanced back later, Martin's usual warm smile had slipped, as though something troubled him. When Anton purposely made eye contact with him again, Martin smiled broadly, shook his head, and held a thumb up to signal his approval. At the other end of the table, after shaking hands with her husband, Bob, Susie ignored his outstretched hand and pulled him into an embrace before whispering in his ear.

"Welcome to the family. I could tell he liked you."

"You could? He certainly had me fooled."

"A sister knows these things. Just be a little patient with him."

"A little patience is something we need from each other right now."

Once they were seated, and at a discreet signal from Martin, waiters came in and arranged *mezze* platters of appetizers along the middle of the table: *dolma*, vine leaves stuffed with lamb; *tzatziki* yoghurt and mint dip; chicken chunks with olive and lemon on skewers; spanakopita delights stuffed in phyllo pastry; chickpea and fennel salad; and baskets of warm pita bread. In between preordered courses, Stephen sat with his arm along the back of Anton's seat and every once in a while placed a hand on Anton's shoulder or stroked a thumb along his neck. Fortified by the gesture, Anton placed his own hand on Stephen's upper thigh and squeezed gently while laughing with Sean and Federico across the table. At one point, as everyone wallowed in cheerful conversation, Anton glanced around the table and felt himself immersed in an overwhelming wave of gratitude at having found these new friends. Only once did he wonder how Christian's evening was going. As soon as desserts had been served and considerable amounts of wine had been consumed, everyone switched places to chat to others around the table, and Anton found a spare seat next to Federico.

"So. You and Stephen, huh? And how did this happen?"

Anton gave him a brief rundown about stopping by to give the doctor presents and then staying for dinner. He omitted mention of anything else, including staying the rest of the weekend.

"So you two have sex already, yes?"

"None of your business!"

"Means yes, then. Good. He seems less—mmm—*enfadado*, angry. He is good at the sack?"

"*In* the sack. He's good *in* the sack."

"Ha!" said Federico, punching his upper arm. "I thought so!"

When he glanced down the table to find Stephen, Martin had cornered him and appeared in the throes of a heated one-way conversation. Anton couldn't see his face, but Stephen's shoulders sagged noticeably. Anton wanted to go over, put his arm around Stephen, and support him. But the two men had a long history, and he didn't want to presume to know better by interfering. Stephen appeared his usual self as the evening drew to a close.

In the taxi on the way back to Anton's apartment, even though they sat nudging shoulders, Stephen remained unusually quiet. Anton twittered on about random conversations that evening while he listened and occasionally smiled. Eventually Anton addressed what he believed to be the root of the silence.

"Martin didn't seem his usual self tonight. Looked as though he was giving you a hard time about something."

"Martin worries too much."

"He cares about you, Stephen."

At that remark, Stephen's gentle gaze settled on Anton.

"Yes, and he cares a lot about you too."

They rode for a time without either of them speaking. Anton wondered what exactly Martin had said but decided not to push the matter. Back in the flat, despite both feeling tired, they made love, and Anton's concerns melted away.

"Before I forget," said Stephen, about to settle down in the bed. "I'll be back in London again in two weeks. Friday the first of December. For the annual medical charity ball in support of World AIDS Day. Black tie and all that nonsense."

"You're more than welcome to stay here with me again. If you want."

"Of course I do. But I was rather hoping you'd accompany me. To the ball."

"As your guest?"

"No," said the doctor, switching the bedside lamp off and pulling Anton in close. "As my boyfriend."

CHAPTER 12
FORGOTTEN

"YOU'VE KNOWN him since when?" came Gemma's voice down the phone.

"October," replied Anton, sighing a steamy breath into the chill night air. Another handsome couple in evening dress glided past and glanced at him as they headed into the warmth and bright lights of the ballroom foyer.

"And you've been together for how long?"

"Three weeks."

"And in those three weeks how many times have you seen each other?"

"Twice," faltered Anton, unable to stop a shiver rattling through his body. "But both times have been amazing. And he's different, Gemma. Even you would like him."

"Thanks for the vote of confidence. You said that about Christian."

"Yes, well, I admit I was wrong about him. I'm not wrong about Stephen."

"Then why are you calling?"

Through the two weeks following the dinner in Wimbledon, small things had begun to eat away at Anton's confidence. Even though they had spoken every other day, Stephen's amorous text messages had dropped off to almost nothing. Work scheduling issues and an overfull appointment diary had forced Stephen to change their Friday night arrangements, and he had called the evening before to say he would drive directly to the venue and meet Anton on the steps outside the Piccadilly Rooms on Charing Cross Road. All week long Anton had been looking forward to enjoying the doctor privately before the event, as well as dusting off and modeling his old evening suit for Stephen to appraise and then helping each other with their troublesome black bow ties and cuff links. Selfish perhaps, but he had been relishing some intimate time before the official event.

"Because I'm going crazy. Because he was supposed to be here at seven."

"So? He's a little late."

"Forty-five minutes. I've been standing in the cold freezing my arse off, looking like a prize penguin. Everyone's staring at me."

"That's because you probably look hot. Have you called him?"

"Twice. Straight to voice mail. And yes, I've left messages. And now my piece of shit phone's telling me I only have 5 percent battery power left."

"So go home."

"I can't. I promised I'd wait for him."

"Then stop complaining. Honestly, Anton, you forget you're not working and have all the time in the world. Poor Stephen is probably busting a blood vessel to get to you. Be a little patient with him if he means that much to you. Call me tomorrow."

As always, his sister provided the indisputable voice of reason, echoing the same sentiment Stephen's sister had made about having patience. Stephen had to drive up directly from his final visit to a hospital in Poole in Dorset, a good two-and-a-half-hour journey in normal traffic. Knowing what the roads on Friday night could be like, he might have met with any number of delays. But please God, thought Anton, let it just be delays and nothing more serious. Anton had experienced Stephen's driving and knew he handled a car with care, certainly safer than Anton. But why couldn't he have taken one minute out of his journey to pull over and call, just to allay Anton's trepidation? Pulling his icy hands from his pockets, he yanked the collar of his overcoat up and bunched the white cashmere scarf into his throat in an attempt to stop the bitter cold from creeping in. Eventually he pulled out a card from his wallet and called Martin, who answered immediately. After brief pleasantries, Anton got down to the point of the call.

"Do you have any idea where Stephen is?"

"Doesn't he have some medical banquet thing in London tonight?"

"With me. But he's not here. Now he's over an hour late, and I'm getting worried."

"Oh, I see." Martin's voice went quiet. "Have you spoken to him at all today?"

"No," said Anton, faltering a moment. "Have you?"

"Not today. But I understand he's been extremely busy."

"Martin, I have to ask. What were you two arguing about at the dinner a couple of weeks ago?"

"It was nothing."

"Rubbish. What were you arguing about?"

At the end of the phone he could hear Martin deciding whether or not to speak, or how much to tell Anton.

"Come on, Martin. I'm a big boy."

After a huge and dramatic sigh, Martin began.

"I told Stephen that he's being selfish. His decision to go to Africa in the New Year is irreversible, and now he's seeing you, singing your praises, and in my opinion, leading you on without thinking about the inevitable consequences. Trust me. Nobody wants him to be happy more than his friends, especially me, but not at someone else's expense and eventual disappointment. You're a lovely man, Anton, but you're vulnerable right now. And it's not your fault. You deserve to be happy too. Your appearance in our lives is a delight. But Stephen has fixed commitments, and he is being an inconsiderate prick getting involved with you."

"I don't mind—"

"Well you *should* mind. You deserve better, Anton."

Maybe from the comment, maybe from the sudden blast of chill air, but Anton felt tears burning his eyes and couldn't respond for a few moments. *How could you get better than the best?* he should have said, but didn't want to argue with Stephen's oldest friend. A soft double beep from his phone warned him the battery was about to fade. He doubted Stephen would be as cruel as Christian and let him down by text message. But after what Martin had just told him, perhaps Stephen was still finding ways to draw things to an end between them. How stupid could he have been, he thought, to believe that someone as professional and together as Stephen could ever really consider out-of-work, insecure Anton as a match.

"Do you think he's still coming?"

"I have no idea. But I don't believe he would abandon you without good cause or without getting word to you first. That's not like him at all. Let me see if I can get hold of him. I'll call you back."

"My battery's almost gone. If he's not here in the next thirty minutes, I'll head home."

"I understand. Let me see what I can find out."

Forty foot-stamping, cheek-freezing minutes passed, and still Stephen had not showed. Anton decided to throw in the towel, and along with his heart and hopes, his phone display finally died. Overworked heaters and cushioned seats in the double-decker bus could do nothing to melt his frozen mood. In fact the amused glances from boarding passengers at his formal attire only made him feel more miserable. For most of the journey he stared out of the window, numb and empty, trying to counter the logical argument that Martin had made. Small things came back to him, such as Stephen's almost dismissive response to his offer of sailing lessons. How could he accept anyway when he would be in Africa? And his silence after Anton's admission to a fear of flying. The relationship was doomed from the start or had come with a very short shelf life. Even so, Anton refused to accept that their connection, their chemistry, had been nothing more than a fling. At least that was certainly not the case for Anton, not in his heart.

On the path leading up to his apartment block, he stopped to view his home and push out a heavy sigh. Strange how a place could transform so quickly from one of safety and security into one that now invoked entrapment. What once had seemed like a safe haven had now become solitary confinement. As he shuffled in resignation toward the door, he slowed his pace on spying the silhouetted bulk of someone or something to the left of the brightly lit entrance. December's winter chill generally forced the homeless into government or charity shelters, or at worst into shop doorways or less exposed hideouts. Cautiously he approached the door, keeping his gaze straight ahead, but as he prodded the entry code on the keypad, a familiar voice croaked from the depths of the bundle.

"Anton."

"Christian? For Christ's sake," said Anton, stumbling back and taking in his ex-lover. By the wan light of the lobby, Anton could just about make out Christian's left eye, dark and swollen almost shut. "What the hell happened?"

As Christian struggled to his feet, Anton strode over and reached to help him.

"Can I come in? I'm freezing my balls off out here," he said, leaning a hand on the glass window to steady himself.

Anton placed a bolstering arm around Christian's back and let the man thrust his arm across Anton's shoulders.

"You're home early for a Friday night," muttered Christian as they negotiated the short distance to the door. "Not that I'm complaining. Thought I would end up freezing to death before you made it home. You being a party pooper?"

"Something like that. Come on. Let's get you upstairs."

"Well, look at you," said Christian as they headed into the block's foyer and Christian got a proper view of Anton's evening suit. "Are you my knight in shining armor? Come to sweep me off my feet?"

A fleeting riposte about someone having already knocked Christian off his feet evaporated when Anton saw the extent of the man's injuries. Apart from the dark red and purple bruising and bloodshot eye, the corner of his mouth was caked with dried blood, and someone or something had provided a nasty and livid graze to his right cheek. Inside the flat, installed on the sofa, his ex would not meet his gaze but instead diverted his attention to the walls. With a gentle shake of his head, Anton strode into the kitchen.

"Nice flat," called Christian. "Like what you've done. Very homey."

When Anton returned with a medical kit and a small pack of frozen peas, he noticed the red light on the answering machine blinking in the corner of the room. Resisting an instant urge to check, he went and stood silently over Christian, forcing the man to meet his gaze.

"We had an argument," said Christian eventually, wincing as Anton guided his hand to press the small frozen pack over his eye. "Max can lose it sometimes. Usually if I mention your name. He gets jealous and flies off the handle easily, especially when he's drunk. Most of the time he's harmless. But it's best to get out of the house when he gets like that."

"Domestic violence is a criminal offence, Christian. You should report this to the police."

"It's not like that. Most of the time he's fine," said Christian, shaking his head softly. "He just has these mad moments."

Anton sighed and sunk down next to him. While he busied himself opening the medical kit and finding what he needed, he sensed Christian watching him.

"Sorry, Ant," he said, leaning his shoulder against Anton's. "I didn't know where else to go."

"If this happens again, I'm taking you straight to the police station."

"If this happens again, you'll probably have to take me to the hospital first," said Christian, chuckling.

"For Christ's sake, Christian," said Anton, mortified. "That's not even remotely funny. How long has this been going on?"

Christian turned away, refusing to answer. Fortunately he had turned his injured cheek toward Anton.

"Hold still. This is going to sting a little."

Anton dabbed a large antiseptic pad on the worst of the abrasion, and as expected, Christian's body stiffened, and he hissed out a sharp breath between his teeth. After a dozen more dabs, Anton felt Christian relax. Satisfied, he closed up the medical kit, then took the phone from his pocket and plugged it into the charger on the coffee table.

"I fucked up, didn't I? We were good together," murmured Christian, a small smile lifting the good side of his mouth.

"Were we? I always thought I disappointed you."

"Not really. Okay, a little, perhaps. Sometimes it felt as though you were only along for the ride. But I had no idea how much I was going to miss you."

Anton let the comment about being along for the ride sink in, trying to make sense of the words. He wondered if he gave Christian the impression of being a passive bystander. Christian often got frustrated by his lack of recklessness, whereas Anton felt that one of them needed to be grounded, to be the adult in the relationship.

"If it's any consolation, I've missed you too."

"Of course you have."

"You want some coffee?"

"Love some. Can I have—"

"Instant. Milk, one sugar."

Christian's soft chuckle sounded as Anton stood up and turned to head for the kitchen. Christian's sudden grasp on his wrist caught him off guard, and he inhaled a breath before being spun around to face Christian.

"Let's try again, Anton."

Anton stared down at the hand clutching his, confused and unable to find words.

"For God's sake, Christian—"

"I missed you. And you've missed me. Yes, I made a mistake because I'm only human. But you *need* me, Anton. What have you been doing this past year? Nothing, according to our friends. Sitting at home, staring at the wall and moping."

Anton's gaze had drifted away from Christian's to his painting of the lonely Newquay landscape on the wall, and then to the other pictures Stephen had helped him hang in the apartment. Before the fateful day he had crashed his car, he would have given anything to have Christian sitting right here and back in his life. But that old ache, that yearning, belonged to a different version of himself. Even with

Stephen cooling off or even gone, he knew he had outgrown that old version, felt much better about himself than he had in years.

"You told me I wasn't enough."

"I…. Things were said in the heat of the moment."

"Texted. You texted those words to me. I still have your message on my phone."

"Said. Texted. Whatever. My mind was all over the place."

"The point is, this is all there is of me, Christian. Nothing more. What you see in front of you is all of me. I am not going to magically transform into some action man just because you realize I'm not so bad after all."

"Don't *say* that. You were as much to blame for the breakup as me, you know. With your total lack of bollocks. You never once asked me *not* to leave, never once fought to keep me. You just let me go."

"And if I had asked you to stay, would you have?"

"Not the point," said Christian, the old familiar anger surfacing once more. "You just accepted it. You're a fucking coward, a defeatist."

"I might not be spontaneous or adventurous—in or out of the bedroom—or whatever kind of crazy you're looking for, but I am not a coward. And I sure as hell never got drunk and knocked you around."

After a deep breath, Christian released his grip on Anton's hand and thrust the same hand into his jacket pocket.

"Be honest," said Anton, the words making him sad but knowing they had to be said. "We had our chance. And you're better off without me. Even if Max is not the answer."

"I suppose this is about that doctor you've been seeing."

Anton frowned, puzzled, wondered for a moment how Christian could know about Stephen. But then he remembered Max meeting them in the street. About to respond, he froze, seeing Christian searching for something on his mobile phone.

"You need to be careful, Anton. Doctor Death, the headlines called him," said Christian, grimacing and holding the phone out to Anton. "Killed his lover. Have you seen this?"

His phone display showed the front page of an online tabloid, the Sunday *Investigator*, with a picture of a flustered Stephen outside a courthouse, grimacing at the camera while shading his eyes from blinding camera flashes. Anton wondered how many photographs they had snapped before they managed to get one so unflattering, bordering on menacing, with Stephen's angry glare accentuating the scar on his face. Even so, a flutter of attraction and excitement trembled in Anton's stomach on seeing the man. As a headline "Doctor Death" was hardly original, but the hook line caught his attention: "NHS doctor, Stephen Miller, the murderer who doles out mercy killings by administering lethal drug doses to defenseless patients, walks away from court released on a technicality." He only skimmed the rest of the article, but the journalist went on to mention Stephen being arrested on suspicion of killing his patient and partner, Sebastian Carerro. As far as Anton could tell, there appeared to be no mention of Sebastian's battle with cancer.

"So he didn't tell you. This is exactly why you need me. Not only are you naive, but you can be incredibly gullible."

"This is bullshit. It has to be."

"So that's *not* him?"

"No. I mean yes, of course that's Stephen. But he's not a criminal," said Anton, floundering. Not for the first time he realized how little he really knew about the doctor. Maybe this was another reason why the man had cooled off, because he didn't want Anton to know about the skeletons in his closet. "You don't know him."

"And you do, I suppose? Come on, Anton. Why else would the police have arrested him? Why else would he have been called to appear in court?"

"How the hell should I know!" shouted Anton, turning on Christian in helpless rage.

Next to him, Christian's features softened, and he gently shook his head.

"Sorry. Maybe I should have kept my mouth shut."

Anton lowered his head, deflated.

"No, you shouldn't. I'm glad you told me. But he's still practicing, so whatever they're saying can't have been proven. Otherwise he would have been struck off the medical register. And his partner, Sebastian, died of cancer, something they carefully neglected to mention. No idea what they mean by a technicality, but you know what the press is like. Anything for a story."

"Well, if it's any consolation, the article is more than two years old. Look, Anton, I know I've let you down once. But I didn't want to see you get hurt again. Do you like him?"

"Yes. At least, I thought I did. I thought we had a connection. But obviously there's a lot about him I don't know. I was supposed to meet him tonight. But he didn't show up."

"He stood you up. Something we're both guilty of, then?" said Christian, chuckling, but then, seeing Anton's pain, he quieted and pulled him down on the sofa next to him. "At least I had the decency to let you know. Even if it was by text message."

"You were always honest and on the level with me when we were together."

"And is that so bad to be around?"

"No, of course not. But come on, Christian, you must have been looking for something more. Otherwise you wouldn't have found Max."

"Max found me."

"Whatever. You found each other. And left me with nothing. I just keep wondering why the hell it's always me."

"What do you mean?"

"Why I'm always the last one to know anything."

"Tell you what," said Christian, putting his hand on Anton's knee. "Let me sort out the coffee. Make myself useful."

While Christian busied himself in the kitchen, talking amiably about one thing or another while opening and closing cupboards, Anton's gaze scanned the room again and came to rest on the answering machine. He had a pretty good idea the message would be from Martin, probably telling him either that he had been unable to find Stephen or that he had spoken and they were over. If it was the latter, he didn't want to hear. But he would never know unless he listened. Moreover, he needed to know nothing bad had happened to Stephen, so after picking up his partially charged mobile phone, he moved across the room, took a deep breath, and pressed the play button.

"…need to fucking cover for him, 'cause I know he's there, Swann" came the slurred voice of Max. Anton was less surprised by Max's voice than by the sudden realization that the man had called his home once before. "Well you can tell him from me to fuck right off. I'm sick of his pathetic games. Always throwing your name in my face if I don't live up to his expectations. Well no more. As soon as the hospital discharges me, I'm moving back in with Rich. Tonight. Tell him, if he's there. What am I saying? Course he's there. He's probably telling you a pack of lies about me right now, 'cause that's what he's good at. Bet he told you I hit him first, didn't he? Outside the pub. Yeah? Course he did. But he's not the one with the broken arm, is he? And ask him where he really was those two weekends at the end of January. When you two were still together and when he told you he was in Birmingham and Manchester for trade shows. Ask him. 'Cause he dragged me down to Hastings. Shagging like rabbits, we were. Both times. Same as the weekend he dumped you. That's the kind of bloke you used to be with—"

Anton punched his fist so hard at the Delete key that he broke the machine.

"He's lying" came Christian's voice from the kitchen door.

"Is he? Is he really, Christian? And why would he bother?"

"Because he wants you to hate me."

"Did you start the fight?"

"What does it matter? I'm here now."

"And how could he know about those two particular weekends? Because you *were* away, for both of them. Attending trade shows, as far as I knew," said Anton, finally looking up and seeing Christian holding a mug and a tea towel and looking suitably guilty. "Were you with him? In Hastings?"

"You don't understand," cried Christian, and for the first time, Anton's own heart tugged at the miserable sound. "Max used to be persuasive. He always got what he wanted. I couldn't say no to him, even though I wanted to. That's why I felt it only fair to break up with you. I didn't want to bring you into that fucked-up situation, knew it wouldn't be fair to ask you to compete for me, especially with someone like Max."

"And you call *me* a coward. You need to go now."

"What? No. Let me stay. Just one night?"

"Go home. Max is no longer there. And I don't want you here."

At least Christian had the decency to look sheepish. On his way past, he stopped and turned slowly at the front door.

"Can I still see you?" he asked. "As friends?"

"Go to hell, Christian."

As soon as the door closed behind him, as soon as the flat fell silent again, Anton slid down the front door to sit on the mat and allowed all of the emotions of the evening to pour out of him in one long, earth-shattering sob. As the tears fell, the mobile in his hand buzzed. On the phone display, the name he had been desperate to see all evening finally appeared.

Stephen.

After staring at the word for a few seconds, feeling the urgent buzz in the palm of his hand, he switched the phone off completely and curled up alone on the mat.

CHAPTER 13
GALLAGHER

TEN DAYS before Christmas, Anton once again found himself in Newquay, this time with the excuse of helping his sister and the kids put up Christmas decorations and also babysitting while Ewan and Gemma attended his work's Christmas party. But from a personal viewpoint, he wanted to get away from his padded cell in Croydon. In the days following the medical ball, Stephen had called a few times, but Anton could not find the strength to answer. A couple of terse messages asking him to call him back had not helped. And by Thursday the calls had stopped altogether. Gallagher had called once too, but he guessed Martin had put him up to that, and he decided not to respond. Strangely enough, an inner peace had settled in Anton, tainted with sadness and disappointment but nothing like the self-loathing that had followed his breakup with Christian. Perhaps he was becoming inured to abandonment.

One thing was certain, the chaos of a weekday morning in Gemma's household left him little time to wallow. He had arrived late the previous evening and had barely said hello to the grown-ups—the kids, Trevor and Clara, already asleep—before being jostled off to bed. That morning, while he sat at the table in his pajamas drinking coffee, Gemma busied herself getting the children ready for school, something Anton learned very quickly to avoid. She had a pseudo-military routine where the little people were concerned, and he only ever spoke to her if spoken to.

"Clara Jane," she hollered from the kitchen doorway. "Go and wake your brother. I want you both down here, washed and changed, in ten minutes flat, or I'm coming up these stairs."

Anton had already learned to tune out these high-octane exchanges between mother and her brood.

"Where did Ewan go?" she asked, her voice instantly back to normal as she returned to ironing her daughter's school blouse while muting the news on the flat screen TV.

"In the garden. Taking a call. Think it's work related."

"It's probably about the party tomorrow tonight. Poor thing. They've had him running around all over the place. Changing this, changing that. He'll be pleased when it's all over and done with."

"He said they're bringing in the whole operation. Top guns, the new subsidiaries and all."

"Trying to bring them all together after the merger. Biggest event they've ever held down this way. Can't do his career any harm, though. He's been invited to attend the executive dinner tonight. First time ever. And then I'm on his arm tomorrow night. We'll try not to be back too late, though."

"Don't worry about me," said Anton. He liked the peace of the house once the kids had gone to sleep. "Go and enjoy yourselves. I'm more than happy staying in with the kids."

He sipped his coffee and flicked through the *Guardian,* but noticed she had stopped ironing.

"Actually, now I've got you alone, there's a couple of things I need to talk to you about. First off, thanks for making the effort with Ewan. It makes such a difference to him. And you two seem to be genuinely hitting it off."

"Turns out we have quite a lot in common." Since their chat in October, they had managed to get along much better, and Ewan always saved up a few jibes about the latest performance of the English rugby team.

"Good. Now, have you spoken to Stephen?"

And there it was. His sister. Straight for the jugular. He groaned inwardly.

"No point now. I've left it too long."

"Don't be ridiculous."

"I am not meant to be in a relationship, Gemma. I'm better off on my own. Better for anyone who gets too close too."

The iron clunked back into the holder.

"For God's sake, Anton. You know you do this, don't you?"

"Do what?"

"Nobody loves you like I do, little brother. But sometimes you drive me to distraction. Finally you've found someone who's worth fighting for. Instead you bury your head in the sand in the hopes that everything will resolve itself around you. Life doesn't work like that. I bet even now you're telling yourself you're not good enough for him."

"That's because I'm not."

"How do you know? Have you even asked him?"

"Doesn't matter. It's too late."

"It's never too late to fight for something you want."

Fortunately at that moment not only did little Clara come screeching into the kitchen in her vest and skirt, telling tales on her brother, but Ewan returned from his phone call.

He appeared suitably rattled, taking Gemma's attention away from Anton.

"Hon, I don't suppose you could take the kids out for breakfast?" he said as she helped little Clara into her school blouse and provided him with a suitably frosty look. "I know, and I don't want to push you out, but Ted phoned to say he's got some big shot from the West Midlands region as well as the new bloody chief exec in tow. They want to have a quick meeting here before we drive to the factory. And I'm going to need a bit of peace and quiet. He's on his way right now."

"I can take them," volunteered Anton before she could muster a response, relieved to be able to get out of Gemma's range of fire. Besides, every now and again he liked to spend time with his nephew and niece and treat them to foods that Gemma barred from the house. "Gemma can stay with you for moral support."

"Oh no, you don't," she said, getting prickly. "I'm not having you stuffing them full of fast food. I'll be the one summoned to the school because they've been bouncing off the walls all morning."

"Think it might be best if you all went," said Ewan, texting on his phone. "Take them to Lucy's on the corner. Give me around thirty to forty-five minutes, and then we'll be out of the house."

"Yay! Lucy's," said Trevor junior, who had turned up during their conversation, dressed and ready. "Blueberry muesli."

"That sounds like a yes," said Gemma before turning to Anton. "The kids are almost ready. How about you? Not coming along in your pajamas, are you?"

"Do I have time to grab a quick shower, Ewan?"

"Sure. If you hurry," said Ewan, checking his watch as Anton began to rise from the table.

"Okay, we'll go ahead and grab a table," said Gemma, herding the kids toward the hallway. "Make sure you come and meet us as soon as you're done. And don't even think we've finished our conversation yet."

Ewan spared Anton a sympathetic shrug as the front door slammed shut. The distant tinkle of laughter sounded as the kids and Gemma headed off down the street, while Anton bounded up the stairs to get ready. After locking the bedroom door—something he always did now, even though Ewan had never paid another visit—and laying out warm clothes on his bed, he dived into the adjoining bathroom. For a change he showered in record time. Once he had toweled himself dry and begun to pull on his clothes, ending with his thick pullover, he heard the distinctive ring of the front doorbell. He cursed under his breath and went to unlock the bedroom door. Downstairs, Ewan's rumbling voice invited someone in. From the sounds of a door sliding to, he assumed Ewan had taken them into the kitchen, which was perfect because Anton could creep down the stairs and slip out of the front door without being seen or heard. After lacing his trainers tight, he crept to the top of the stairs and began the slow descent. Halfway down the stairs the kitchen door slid open, and at the sound of a warmly familiar voice, Anton froze.

"...plant production is excellent—of all this region's factories, yours seems to be the shining star—so I wanted to see for myself how the new processes you've put in place are working, see if we can adopt any in my region. Hope that's okay with…."

As the man turned to look up at Anton, a moment of almost comical freeze-frame occurred, with Anton's jaw dropping open, his mind unable to find a voice. Ewan jumped in nervously to introduce the men to each other.

"This is Anton, my brother-in-law. He's staying with us for the Christmas holidays. Anton, these are my colleagues, Ted Hopkins, my regional manager, and his counterpart from the West Midlands region—"

"Gallagher," said Anton finally. "How have you been?"

Before Gallagher, who appeared as stunned as Anton, could find words to respond, a third figure stepped forward, surprising everyone.

"Well fuck me sideways, Anton Swann," said William J. Mitchell, CEO of the Masblock Corporation. "Where the devil have you been hiding? We've dropped Mitfords from our legal panel, you know. The last team they sent us didn't know their arses from their elbows. Your head of corporate, Pete Burke, told me you'd resigned."

"They let him go, Bill," said Gallagher finally. "This is the young man I've been telling you about. How the hell do you know him?"

"If you'd mentioned his name, I would have told you straightaway," said Bill.

"Anton?" asked Ewan.

Anton almost felt sorry when he saw the baffled face of his brother-in-law, looking from Gallagher to Bill Mitchell and then back to Anton.

"It's okay, Ewan. We worked together on the acquisition of Pinnacle Plastics. Back when I was an associate with Mitfords. In London," said Anton, bewildered himself by the unusual tableau of familiar faces. "Back in 2012."

"And let me tell you," said Bill, folding his arms. "This young man is a bloody marvel to have on your side. Worked his arse off for us, he did. Stopped a couple of meetings from going into meltdown. For

Christ's sake, Gallagher, snap the boy up already. Before somebody else beats us to it. Ted, and Ewan and I will be having a confab in the front room."

Even as the men filtered into the room and shut the door, Anton and Gallagher stayed where they were. And then suddenly a wave of emotion overtook Anton and he raced down the stairs to give Gallagher a fierce hug. On his part Gallagher not only accepted the embrace but reciprocated. Only as they pulled apart did Anton realize tears had started to fill his eyes.

"Hey, hey," said Gallagher, squeezing his upper arms. "Let's go and sit in the kitchen."

"I didn't know you worked for Masblock," said Anton as they perched on kitchen seats.

"Officially, I don't. But our companies fall under the same umbrella. I tried to get hold of you about this job. Left a message. Assumed you weren't taking calls right now, after what Martin said. Anyway, to keep things aboveboard, I'll need your résumé and for you to meet our head of legal in London. Mind you, if Bill wants you on board then that's purely academic. Just in time too, because we've got a couple of huge projects coming up down this way in January. How do you fancy a move?"

"Where to?"

"Our southwest office is in Plymouth. For the most part you'd be working out of there. Maybe a couple of days a month in London. Means you'd be nearer here, nearer your family. How does that sound?"

"I don't know what to say," he said, imagining Gemma's reaction.

"Then say yes, for goodness' sake. Otherwise Bill will have my head on a plate."

With his business head on, Gallagher went on to explain the job and some of the more significant upcoming projects. Anton sat stunned, listening to the man he saw as a friend talk knowledgeably and enthusiastically about how and where Anton would be involved. After touching on the not insignificant remuneration and benefits,

Gallagher pulled out his smartphone and, while sitting there, not only agreed on a date for Anton to meet their head of legal and the recruitment person in their London office, but fired off an e-mail to make all the arrangements. When he finished, Gallagher sat there grinning until Anton finally changed the topic.

"Have you spoken to Stephen?"

"Ah," said Gallagher, his smile slipping. "Now for some tough love."

"Oh God, Gallagher. I've made such as mess of things, haven't I? Even my sister gave me a piece of her mind this morning. But I thought maybe he'd had a change of heart. And someone showed me the headline of a newspaper. Had a photograph of Stephen being arrested for killing a patient. It looked like Sebastian—"

"Oh, for crying out loud. Is that going to haunt Stephen forever? Yes, Sebastian took an overdose to end his life rather than continue suffering. Stephen wasn't even there at the time. It was when the night nurse was caring for him. But Stephen had usually administered the pills, a part of Sebastian's prescription, and he always left them near the bed. That night, while the nurse wasn't watching, Sebastian took the overdose. The police had to be called, and they took Stephen in for questioning on suspicion of assisted suicide. Of course they had no proof whatsoever, and once Stephen's solicitor arrived, they let him go. But someone alerted the gutter press—possibly the nurse—and they ran a story that said Stephen had killed his patient. Poor bastard, grieving the loss of Sebastian and had all that bullshit to deal with as well."

"Gallagher, honestly, I never knew. I should have answered his call. But I assumed he'd cooled off that night."

"Then you clearly don't know Stephen. Martin told me you called him. In fairness, none of us could get hold of him."

"And then my phone died."

"Martin blames himself. And to be honest Stephen blamed him too. Eventually they had a blazing row over the phone. He thinks Martin scared you off. Thank goodness they're both thick skinned, especially with everything else going on."

"Martin was just being honest."

"But Stephen was beside himself because he couldn't get word to you. Everything went to hell that night. Having to deal with the death of his father."

"What?" asked Anton, horrified.

"Oh, Lord, you didn't know," said Gallagher, releasing a huge groan. "What a mess. The night of the medical ball, the reason he didn't turn up is because his father had another stroke. Far more serious this time. He didn't last the night. They buried him the Wednesday just gone."

Tears blurred Anton's vision then, his head falling into his hands. Once again he had completely misjudged the situation because he hadn't bothered to call back and find out. His sister was right. He'd buried his head in the sand. Just like he always did. And Stephen would have needed him by his side. Maybe the doctor was better off without him.

"I've fucked up, haven't I?"

"Only one way to find out, old man."

Anton rested his forehead on the bay window of Gemma and Ewan's house, watching the men drive away in Ted's Mercedes. He and Gallagher had promised to stay in touch this time, not only about the job, and Anton had given his word that he would call Martin, as soon as a few other things had been resolved. Gemma was right. He needed to grow up and fight. Not try to convince himself of the freedom of an uncomplicated, single, but ultimately selfish independence, when all the time what he really craved was a relationship, with all its messiness and compromise but incomparable rewards. After calling Gemma's mobile phone and explaining briefly what had happened, he took a few steadying breaths and dialed an all-too-familiar number. After the phone had rung six times, Anton almost lost his nerve and replaced the receiver, but right then a familiar voice answered.

"Doctor Miller" came Stephen's professional voice, a little out of breath.

Anton gulped once to try and steady his nerves before speaking. "Stephen, this is Anton."

Silence was followed by a small, barely audible sigh.

"Yes, Anton," replied the equally professional but somewhat cold voice.

"I'm sorry. If this is a bad time, I can call back."

"I'm in the middle of packing. So if you have something to say, you'd better speak now. I'm flying out today. To Ghana."

Anton placed his forehead into his free hand, his heart sinking. Too late. He was too late.

"I thought you weren't leaving until the New Year."

Despite the sob inside trying to escape, he succeeded in keeping emotion from his voice.

"The charity administrators called to say they're short staffed over the holiday season. Asked if I could start early. I saw no reason to turn them down."

They had planned to spend time together over the Christmas season, but then Anton had disappeared off the radar. Why would Stephen need to stick around? In the hope that Anton might call? Of course not, Anton had seen to that.

"I just—I spoke to Gallagher. He told me what happened. Everything. And I wanted to phone and talk to you. Oh God, Stephen. I don't know where to begin."

"Look, Anton. I appreciate your call. I really do. But I've got a number of things to sort out before the taxi arrives."

"I understand," said Anton quietly. "Maybe it's best I let you go."

"Yes, probably right," said Stephen, but he remained on the line.

Anton took this as a good sign and pressed Stephen for more details.

"How long will you be gone?"

"Initially one year, realistically two."

"So you've sold the house."

"No, I took her off the market. Want to keep a foothold in the country. For whenever I return."

"I see. Will you get any time off?"

"One weekend a month. Not long enough to fly home. But I'll have a week's holiday in June."

"At least that's something. Where are you flying out from? Today?"

"Heathrow. Four thirty. Taxi's coming at midday."

Anton faltered then, the sudden realization of Stephen's departure hitting him hard.

"I need to see you. Before you go."

"Anton, I don't think that's a good—"

"Please. If I leave here now, I can be with you by ten."

"Anton—"

"*Please*. There's so much that needs to be said. Just wait for me," said Anton before putting down the phone, grabbing his car keys, and hurrying out the front door.

CHAPTER 14
FAREWELL

THE FIRST thing Anton noticed when he pulled up outside the coach house was the absence of the For Sale sign. At another time the sight might have made him feel better. On his drive up, the sky had become progressively overcast, with thick, dark clouds gathering, and now lights blazed inside the house. Almost as soon as he had turned out of Gemma's road, he began rehearsing in his head what he needed to say. But by the time he pulled into the familiar lane, most of the words had become scrambled in overriding emotions. He switched off the engine and took a few settling breaths before climbing out of the car.

"Come inside," called Stephen, who had opened the front door as soon as Anton placed a hand on the garden gate. Anton noticed immediately how the doctor avoided eye contact and spoke with none of the warmth of their last meeting. Inside the threshold, a huge aluminum suitcase and a black leather medical bag lay to one side of the door. Stephen ushered Anton into the living room and, after closing the door, came and stood across the room from him. For a moment Anton considered sitting but instead turned to address Stephen while scraps of words remained fresh in his mind. Before he had a chance, however, the doctor began speaking.

"Before you say anything, I need to make it perfectly clear that I don't blame you for anything. I was being completely selfish," he said, his voice carrying the professional detachment of his vocation. "Martin was right. We should never have started anything. I'm going to be away for at least a year, for God's sake. That's not fair on you."

"I already knew," said Anton quietly. "Your sister told me at the hospital."

An awkward silence hung in the air between them. Anton brimmed with things he wanted to say, but he didn't know how to begin, didn't trust the maelstrom of emotions swirling away inside him. Stephen's coolness unnerved him. Once again, Stephen was the first to break the silence.

"The cab will be here in a couple of hours," said Stephen, planting his hands in his jacket pockets. "Say what you came here to say."

Anton winced at the directness and stared away. When his thoughts became words, they tumbled out angry and disjointed.

"Why didn't you tell me you'd been plastered all over the front page of a newspaper?" he cried. "We said no secrets, remember?"

"Newspaper?" said Stephen, confused and then becoming incensed. "Is that what this was about? Muckraking fabrication in that piece-of-shit tabloid. Did you also know they printed an apology after my father successfully sued them for libel?"

"But you didn't tell me," cried Anton. "I had to find out from Christian."

"That happened two years ago. And it's not exactly something I want to dig up, let alone discuss. How the hell did Christian find out?"

"I don't know. Max, probably," said Anton. And in that moment it dawned on him. Max had recognized Stephen the night they met on the street in Wimbledon, probably remembered the article. He would have relished digging up dirt and telling Christian the whole sordid story. Little knowing the ploy to make Anton look pathetic had actually backfired and brought Christian to his door.

"What are you saying? That you believed the article?" said Stephen, hurt showing in his eyes. "You really think that's the kind of person I am?"

"No, of course not. But at the time I didn't know what to believe."

"Then why didn't you pick up the phone and ask me?"

"I know. I should have done that. I'm sorry, okay?" said Anton, hating himself for becoming defensive. "I was hurt and angry. For many reasons. You left me standing outside the hall in London in the cold looking stupid. For over an hour. All my calls went to voice mail. I didn't know what to think. The last time something like that happened was when Christian dumped me."

Standing outside Waterloo Station after work that Friday night, with two first class tickets for a weekend break to Paris on the Eurostar. Until Christian's now-infamous breakup text had arrived. He never wanted to feel like that ever again.

"My father—" began Stephen softly.

"Yes, I know *now*. Gallagher told me," said Anton, and then more gently added. "And I can't begin to tell you how truly sorry I am. I should have been there for you. By your side."

Stephen sighed then and lowered himself down on the arm of the settee. When Anton dared to glance over at him, his posture had the look of the defeated, head hanging low between his shoulders.

"Can't you see it's better this way, Anton?" said Stephen eventually, his voice calm again. "Nobody gets hurt. We go our separate ways and get on with our very different lives."

Anton felt sick, the vein in his neck pounding.

"Is that what you want?" he asked quietly, staring down at the floor.

"I think it's for the best, don't you?" said Stephen, softening his tone. "But we can at least remain friends, can't we?"

Anton felt his stomach clenching, his throat tightening, unable to bring himself to speak.

"Can we?" said Stephen.

On the day Christian had broken up with him, he had accepted it without a fight and gone into hiding. Misery and self-loathing became a way of life, haunting every minute of every hour, wasted emotions and time he could never get back. And at their last meeting, when Anton finally realized he no longer trusted nor desired him, Christian had asked to stay friends and Anton had told him to go to hell. But Stephen was different, genuine, not a duplicitous cell in his body. He would be a true and loyal friend.

"I can't," said Anton eventually, the whispered words bursting from him.

"Why not?" said Stephen, the hurt clear in his voice.

174

"Because I love you," he blurted, hugging himself, the tears finally brimming over despite his best efforts to hold them back, "and it would kill me to be around you as just a friend."

"Oh God, Anton," said Stephen, standing up and striding across the room to clasp him in his arms. Anton pushed his damp face into the shoulder of the doctor's jacket and wrapped his arms tightly around his waist. After a moment Stephen pulled Anton's head away and rested his hands either side of his face until Anton looked into his eyes.

"I do," said Anton miserably, tears falling. "I mean it."

"I know you do," said Stephen warmly, brushing a thumb beneath each of Anton's eyes to wipe away the tears, his gentle, humorous expression melting into one of tenderness. "And I love you too."

With that Stephen kissed him firmly, with something already resembling familiarity, his mouth a smile, and Anton met the embrace wholeheartedly, the tension in his body finally breaking. Straight afterward, Anton placed his head on Stephen's shoulder and sighed deeply, enjoying the simple pleasure of being held. Something strange happened then. With his eyes half-closed, Anton wondered if the tears had blurred his vision or whether the lights in the room had flickered. He squeezed the tears from his eyes and opened them again just as the room became dark.

"Perfect," huffed Stephen, staring at the ceiling but not letting Anton go. "Another power outage."

But for Anton, a sudden calm had enveloped him, a sensation like the one he had experienced the day his car crashed into the wall, which had immersed him in an intimate and overwhelming feeling of well-being. His head fixed in place on Stephen's shoulder, his gaze focused on a misty figure in the corner of the room, leaning back into the window frame, one leg crossed in front of the other. Clearer than ever now was the grinning figure of Sebastian, a lit cigarette dangling from his mouth. While gazing on, he gave Anton two thumbs up. After retrieving the cigarette with one hand, he pointed to it with the forefinger of the other before pressing the same finger over his lips. Their secret. Finally he stubbed the cigarette repeatedly into the cup of his hand while winking once at Anton. Smoke rose from the palm and began to mingle with his form, until all that remained of Sebastian were the ghostly tendrils wafting out through the seams of the windowpanes and out into the darkened sky. As quickly as they had cut, the lights flickered back on again.

Of course. Everything made sense now. Sebastian had been in the bedroom his first night in the coach house, had been standing by the window observing him. And at the bedroom window the afternoon Stephen's car had broken down. Anton wondered if Sebastian's ghost had tampered with Stephen's car and the house phone. No way of knowing for sure, but that evening had cemented Anton's feelings for Stephen. Had that been Sebastian's intention all along? To bring the two of them together? In which case, his work was done, leaving Anton with the greatest gift of all, standing right there in front of him, in his arms.

When Anton tightened his hold on Stephen, the doctor first kissed his neck and then began to whisper in his ear.

"The smell of a home-cooked dinner. When I walk up the gravel pathway to the front door of this house."

"Sorry?" Anton whispered back, confused, but Stephen continued on.

"Second, barely being able to hold myself together when I have to face family members of patients, to give them bad news. Three, the way your eyes open wide and you make that little surprised gasp when we're making love. That's a new one. Four, that I also want to have kids one day. Right now more than ever."

"And five?" said Anton, grinning broadly against the doctor's neck.

"That I like surprises. Good ones. I know you don't, but I love them. And you, Anton, are the biggest and best surprise of all."

Stephen began to pull Anton in for another kiss, but Anton stopped him with a hand on his chest.

"How much packing do you have left?"

"All done, baby," said Stephen, stroking Anton's face. He seemed content for them to stand in the middle of the room, clinging to each other until the taxi arrived.

"In which case, can we go upstairs one last time?"

"I would very much like that," said Stephen, grinning before leaning in and gently nipping Anton's lower lip, "but as time is pressing, I think you're going to have to skip the trailers."

ANTON CROUCHED over Stephen and accepted him because he wanted to brand to memory every expression, every movement, and every sound as they made love. They moved with familiarity and precision, lips fused together, Stephen's cock sliding in and out of Anton to the rhythm of their carnal dance. Every touch, every stroke of flesh brought Anton's body to life, as though Stephen had memorized a secret map of his body, one he had studied meticulously. Eventually they collapsed together, resting in each other's arms, breathing heavily but both cocooned in each other's love and body warmth.

"Am I forgiven?" asked Anton.

"Nothing to forgive. We both made mistakes."

Metallic ticks from Anton's wristwatch on the bedside cabinet counted down the seconds, something they both noticed with sadness. They lay facing each other, their hot breath mingling, caressing the skin of each of their damp faces.

"I was almost there, you know," said Stephen. "That night of the ball. Had made really good progress. About half an hour away when the call came through. I thought it was you, but when I pulled over and answered, the first thing I saw was that the phone hadn't been charging. I usually do that in the car between visits. But for some reason the cable hadn't worked all the way from Poole. Luckily I managed to get one call in to hear the news and tell them I was on my way before the phone gave out. After plugging and unplugging a dozen times, I swore at the cable and then shouted at the car—because that kind of thing always works. And then I remembered what you said to me when my father had his first stroke, that I should be with family, that it's what you would have wanted if it had been you. And you know, your words comforted me then. I didn't reach Plymouth Royal until almost nine o'clock and handed my phone to the attendant on the ward. They know me there. After that I've no idea where time went. We were all at his bedside when he died. Mum, Susanna, and I. Although he didn't regain consciousness."

"You didn't get to say good-bye?"

"Funny, you know. I think I did. I made a habit of calling every morning to find out how he was doing. Usually Mum answered and gave me the news. He hated the fuss. But that very morning he picked up for a change. We did the usual checklist of medicines and exercise. And as usual he humored me. But as we were about to say our good-byes he suddenly came out with. 'Son, I hope you know how much I love you and how proud I am of who you are.' It stopped me in my tracks for a moment, and I'm glad I told him I loved him too."

Both remained still then, pondering what Stephen had said.

"I'm not sure I even phoned you that night," said Stephen.

"You did. But I was having my own meltdown."

When Stephen turned his head to Anton, waiting for him to go on, Anton gently shook his head.

"Not important. Another time. Look, Stephen, I know you're committed to this stint in Africa, and I respect that," said Anton, happily letting Stephen nestle his head in the crease between his arm and his shoulder. "Although I'm a little surprised Susanna is letting you go before Christmas."

"Her and Mum weren't over the moon. But the charity is desperate, Anton. Genuinely. This work is not like a normal job. It's not like running my own rural medical practice here and seeing patients, most of whom have minor afflictions. Children are dying every day there. With diseases people in this country will probably never have to face. This charity is a lifeline for the people in that part of Ghana, offering practical medical help and sourcing funding for vital medicines. Oddly enough, my mum clinched it. She said not only would my father have told me to go, but that also, once I make my mind up to do something, I never back down."

"Stubborn?"

"Committed."

"It's one of the things I love about you. And I didn't come here to talk you out of anything or change any plans. But I want you to know that I *am* going to be here for you."

"Anton—"

"I *am*. But only if you want me to," said Anton, kissing the top of his head.

"Of course I want you to," said Stephen. "It just doesn't seem fair to you."

"In which case, you may want to hear my terms and conditions."

"Oh dear. Is this the out-of-work lawyer speaking? Am I going to like this?"

"For starters, you phone me at least once a week. Or if it's easier, give me a number in Ghana and a time, and I'll call you. FaceTime or something similar, if possible."

"Deal. I'll need to get myself established, but I promise to sort that out. Next?"

"Before coming here, I met Gallagher. It's a long story, but his company is offering me a job as one of their in-house legal counsel. Starting in January. The only issue is that I'd be working in Plymouth. So I would need to find somewhere to live down this way, preferably somewhere quiet and familiar but somewhere commutable each day, such as—"

"Here?" asked Stephen, swinging his quizzical gaze to Anton.

"I would be earning again so could afford to pay you a modest rent. And pay all the bills, of course. But the office is only about an hour's drive from here."

"Here? Are you serious?" said Stephen, sitting up then and staring, amazed, at Anton. "You would stay here and look after the house for me? And don't even think about rent. I was going to leave the place empty."

"Which is wrong in so many ways. And maybe in my spare time I can finally finish off decorating those rooms you've been meaning to get around to. You said yourself that I'm pretty handy with a paintbrush."

"But are you going to be all right here on your own?"

"It's good enough for you, isn't it? Anyway, I won't be on my own. Everywhere I look I'll see reminders of you," said Anton and almost mentioned Sebastian's name too, although he had a feeling he had seen the last of the resident ghost. Most importantly, being alone in the coach house would be different, in a house he had only ever associated with warm memories and love. "And I know you won't be back until June—when, incidentally, I want you all to myself—but I still want to invite your friends and family over for the weekend now and again. You've created a tradition of sorts, and I want to carry that on for you, for us. And when that happens we'll call you using an online conferencing system. If we can get a connection."

"What about your place in Croydon?"

"With the recent makeover, I could rent it in a heartbeat."

Next to him, Stephen had suddenly gone still, and Anton turned to see him deep in thought.

"What did I ever do to deserve you, Anton Swann?"

"I think you've got that the wrong way around. I just regret that I never got to meet your father."

"Me too," Stephen sighed. "He would have liked you. No more regrets, though."

"No more regrets."

Before they showered, Anton cancelled the taxi cab, insisting on driving Stephen to the airport in his BMW. Stephen had been unsure, but Anton persisted, even phoning the company himself and making up a cock-and-bull story about the flight being canceled. Part of him wished it had been. Stephen gave Anton a set of house keys and ran through instructions for the alarm system and household routines. Before they left, both of them spoke to a very relieved Martin, and Anton agreed to come over and stay with him and Gallagher for a few days during Christmas and the New Year.

"And make sure you write as well," said Anton, bringing the BMW to a halt at a roundabout off the motorway before signaling left. "I don't want to be sitting at home worrying about you every day."

"Yes, mother. I just hope I'll be able to plug in my computer there," said Stephen, grinning at Anton's serious face.

"Write me letters, I mean," said Anton, turning into the lane. "Not just e-mails. I want to know everything."

"If you can decipher them," said Stephen, continuing to smile happily. For almost the whole journey he had rested his right hand on Anton's upper thigh. "You must have heard about doctors' handwriting. And I have no experience of the postal system in Ghana, so I might be back before any letters have even reached you."

Despite Stephen's objections, Anton insisted on parking in the short stay car park to see him off. The doctor suggested they make their proper good-byes still in the front seat of the car before getting the luggage from the boot, a heartfelt kiss and a promise to stay in touch. Together they strolled from the car park to the terminal building, bumping shoulders and unspeaking, Anton grateful to encounter only shops and check-in counters—not a single terrifying air machine in sight. His only regret was in not being able to hold Stephen's hand as they moved forward together.

As he waited to one side while Stephen flirted amiably with the female counter staff, checking in his huge case and collecting his ticket, Anton should have felt sad, should have felt desolate losing the person he had earlier declared his love for. Instead he felt nothing but pride. He would make this work, he told himself, somehow. Because that's what you do when you love someone. There were going to be challenges, of course there were, but already the approaching year seemed more optimistic than the one coming to a close. Only as they stood facing each other before the immigration door, before the long queue and hubbub of people waiting to head to their departure gates, did Anton swallow back a wave of sadness. Although it felt awkward and unnatural, Anton held out his hand to Stephen in a show of public affection, and they stood with hands clasped like businessmen.

"Be strong," said Stephen, smiling into Anton's eyes with so much love.

"I will. And promise me you'll be safe," said Anton, grinning back, tears in his eyes.

Eventually they released their grasp, and Anton stood by as Stephen moved slowly, painstakingly, along the queue. Every few seconds he turned back to smile at Anton until he had almost reached the doorway of no return.

"Stephen," called out Anton, ignoring the queue and striding up to him. As he neared, the doctor's face became alarmed, until Anton reached out, pulled him close, and kissed him full on the lips. Stephen's smile felt wonderful through the kiss as he tightened his arms around Anton, and the people standing nearby let out a gentle "Whoo-hoo."

"Don't ever forget," he whispered into the doctor's ear. "I'll be right here. And even though I'm going to miss you like crazy, it's good to have you back."

Epilogue
Courage

NOT UNTIL the Boeing's wheels had smoothed to coasting along the runway and the jet engines had stopped roaring did Anton lessen his white-knuckled grip on the arms of the seat. In fact, between the moment of the pilot's announcement about descending into Kotoka Airport and touchdown, he felt sure he had barely taken a breath. Since leaving Heathrow Airport six hours ago, neither the airline entertainment system nor the two generous measures of gin and tonic— he'd had no stomach for a meal—could divert his paranoid attention from any foreign noise: a variation in the sound of the engines, the dull ping of seat belt signs being switched on, the vacuumed flush of the plane's toilets. Most of those around him had slept throughout the overnight flight. Apart from waking briefly to re-clasp her belt and straighten her seat, the cheerful Ghanaian woman next to him slept still—or at least had her eyes closed.

"Ladies and gentlemen, welcome to Kotoka Airport, Accra. It has been our pleasure having you on board this flight from London to Ghana. Please remain seated with your seat belt fastened until the plane has come to a complete stop."

When Anton peered down the aisle, he saw the female cabin crewmember nodding encouragingly back at him. Four times during the night she had stopped to ask him cheerfully if he needed anything: a blanket, a cup of tea, a sandwich, or another alcoholic drink. Somebody—probably his sister, who had not only booked him on the flight but had also enrolled him in a one-day "Fear of Flying" course operated by the airline—must have informed them about the chronic aerophobia of this first-time flyer. Gemma had even given him antidepressants to help calm his nerves, but he had been determined to do this properly, naturally, because he felt it would be the only way to move forward. Despite everyone's kind concern, all he genuinely wanted now was to be out of the metal canister and standing safely on solid ground.

Most importantly, though, he had arrived. And he had done so by himself.

During various phone calls and in letters, Stephen had mentioned that Africa smelled like no place on earth, and as Anton stepped out of the immigration hall, out through the official doors into the sunshine of a March morning, he understood exactly what the doctor meant. Apart from the smells of smoked fish and pungent citrus fruits from the early-bird hawker stalls, even the air smelled different, scorched and dusty but with a musky tang.

After a quick gulp of water from his bottle, he set about trying to find his ride. Thirty to forty dark-skinned faces peered at him, holding up name cards, none of which had his name on them. Eventually he found his driver, a cheerful Ghanaian man, carrying a cardboard placard with his name scrawled in green felt pen. Anton was relieved to find that he spoke fluent English.

"Kumasi is three hours, more or less," said the man called Tom, insisting on carrying Anton's small holdall. "But do not worry. I have air-conditioning, good music, bottled water, and we can stop for a toilet break behind a tree whenever you want."

After sitting in busy airport traffic, navigating the roads around the terminal, they eventually settled in at a steady speed on the dual lane highway, which took them directly toward Accra and the heart of Kumasi. Outside the car window, traffic signage and road design were not dissimilar to those in England. For some reason, Anton had expected them to drive on the left hand side of the road, but Ghanaians drove on the right, similar to continental Europe, even though Tom told him that Ghanaians drove wherever they could find a space. Other things were wildly different too: lush green vegetation and alien looking trees that lined the road; lorries overloaded with goods or, on occasion, workers, the tailpipes spewing toxic brown exhaust; women walking casually along the hard shoulder with baskets of goods piled high on their heads, oblivious to the heavy traffic. Tom turned out to be a good driver, not tempted to match the breakneck pace of some of the taxis and other vehicles that passed them. In spite of his fascination with the countryside, within fifty minutes Anton found his head lolling against the window, and before long, he had dropped off to sleep.

Only as they reached the outskirts of Kumasi, as the car slowed to negotiate smaller roads, did he wake to find them approaching the entrance to the Ghana International Relief Center. After a brief chat with a grinning Tom, confirming again that he had the return cab ride arranged, he paid up and bid the man farewell. Bag in hand, he stood staring up at the signage, wondering not for the first time what on earth he had been thinking. Pushing himself forward, he found his way into the small official reception area, currently empty apart from two ladies in medical uniforms sitting at a desk.

"Can I help you?" said the first nurse without looking up from her paperwork.

"I'm here to see Doctor Miller," said Anton to the top of the woman's head.

"Is he expecting you?" asked the woman.

"Actually, no," said Anton, faltering, realizing again how spontaneous and completely out of character his plan had been, and anxious now that his surprise might backfire. Finally the nurse peered up at him.

"I'm a friend of his from England," he continued. "If I could just speak to—"

"Anton. You are Anton," she said, waving the eraser end of her pencil at him and finally breaking into a generous smile that lit up her whole face. The nurse next to her looked over at that and chuckled too. "Oh my. You will give him the shock of his life. Follow me."

She led him through the charity's compound, rows of small mud-brick dwellings and occasional canvas tents housing families, where children of all ages played together. Some, painfully malnourished but all smiling despite their hardship, ran over to grab Anton's hand and pull at his jacket sleeve for attention. One small boy insisted on being picked up, and the nurse stood by patiently while Anton did as asked and had a brief conversation about English football with the youngster. Boldly, the small child introduced himself as Charles and listed names of European footballers, most of whom Anton had never heard, but they both laughed together about more famous names. After a few moments, the nurse pulled the boy off, shooed the children away, and then led him to a private, cordoned-off part of the site.

"He has made such a difference, you know. We are so pleased he came to us. He is sorting out inventory this afternoon, which is not his most favorite job. Sit here in the shade while I go and fetch him," said the nurse, indicating the simple wooden bench beneath the umbrella branch network of a beautiful acacia tree.

Five minutes later, Stephen stepped out of the brick building alone, wearing light blue medical scrubs. Apart from needing a shave and looking a little tired, he seemed alert but had an impatient frown on his face. He wiped his hands on a small towel while scanning the area from left to right. Anton, anxious for a second that he had disturbed him from something urgent, stood up and called his name. When Stephen placed a hand across his eyes to block the sunlight and spotted Anton, his grimace turned to disbelief.

"What on earth are you doing here?" he said, striding over, his bewilderment transforming into a broad smile.

"You said on the phone Monday that you had this weekend off. But if you've got other plans, I can head back," said Anton. "Although you might need to give me something pretty bloody strong to get me back on that plane."

"You flew here?" said Stephen, amazed.

"Apparently it's too far to jog. And let me tell you, my heart almost stopped beating every time we hit a pocket of turbulence. Any chance of a hug?"

"Look at you," said Stephen, stepping forward and pulling him into a tight embrace. "My big man. Facing his fears head on."

"Amazing what can be achieved with the right incentive," said Anton, nuzzling Stephen's neck and breathing in his scent. "God,

I've missed you. Phobia or no phobia, I couldn't last until June. I'm having withdrawal symptoms."

"I can't believe you flew," said Stephen, releasing him and stepping back.

"Me neither," said Anton. "Honestly, though, it wasn't as bad as I'd feared. Hey, how come the nurse at the front desk knew me?"

"Did she now?" said Stephen, smirking and glancing back at the building. "Gloria's a piece of work. All she told me was that a VIP had arrived to see me urgently. She wouldn't say any more. But she knows you. They all do. They've seen the photos Martin e-mailed of us both. From the restaurant. We live in each other's pockets around here, so nothing stays secret for very long."

They strolled along the avenue together, bumping shoulders in their old familiar way, Stephen talking animatedly about the environment he worked in. His enthusiasm for the place shone through like the untarnished sun.

"Actually, I wanted to discuss something over the phone," said Stephen, stopping to face Anton, his face becoming serious. "During our next call. But now seems like the perfect opportunity. It's about my visit back to England in June."

"Why? What is it?"

"Uh," sighed Stephen, staring at the ground. "This is a little delicate."

"What's the matter?" said Anton, his smile dropping. "No, Stephen, please don't say you can't come back. I've already booked the time off work. And we're planning a big party—"

"Anton," said Stephen, smiling gently, a hand on his shoulder, cutting him off. "Will you *please* give me a chance to speak?"

"Sorry," said Anton, his brows scrunched up and gaze fixed on a spot on the ground until Stephen reached over and lifted his face by the chin.

"Since I've been working here, I've spent countless hours alone, especially in the evenings or during the night, and I've had plenty of time to think. And it's made me realize just how lucky I am. More than that, though, I think for the first time I've come to appreciate how precious life is, but also how fragile it can be, and how we have to cling to what we love because it could all end in a heartbeat. So what I'm trying to say in my rather long-winded way is, would you let me make an honest man of you?"

"Sorry?" said Anton. "I don't understand."

"In June. When I'm back. Will you marry me? Please don't make me get down on one knee. Not here. The ground's filthy."

Anton stared on in shock. Until the reality sank in and his fraught features melted.

"Oh my God, yes. Of course, yes. I didn't know what you—Yes!"

"Good," said Stephen, pulling him into a powerful hug until both of their bodies had relaxed. "Actually, love, I need to get back to work and finish—"

"Of course you do. Don't worry about me. I'll find somewhere to hang out until you're done," said Anton, and then as a moment of doubt surfaced, added, "You do still have the weekend off, don't you?"

"I'm supposed to finish around six," said Stephen, nodding. "Although to be honest, if you weren't here I might have given it a miss again, we're so shorthanded. But Gloria insisted and booked me into a lodge in the next village, an hour's drive away. Other workers recommended the place for some rest and relaxation. Nothing luxurious, but hot water, good food, and a comfortable bed."

"And me," said Anton.

"And now you," said Stephen, grinning happily. "A very welcome bonus."

"Soundproofing?"

"Supposedly private self-contained chalets," said Stephen before lowering his voice. "But we have to be discreet. Ghana isn't as liberal as merry old England."

"After traveling three thousand miles to find you, I'll be anything you need me to be," said Anton.

"Good answer," said Stephen, laughing and squeezing his upper arm. "While I finish up, I'll get someone to take you to my room. Get yourself some shut-eye. You look tired. And I want you wide awake tonight."

Stephen lived in a small concrete hut in the compound, barely larger than a garden shed. A single bunk took up most of the space, but a couple of make-do shelves had been fixed into the wall to house Stephen's medical books, and a low, rickety table of rattan stood next to the bed. No wardrobe or drawers could fit into the space, and Anton assumed that Stephen lived out of his suitcase. Apart from being a single occupancy room, he also had the benefit of a washbasin in the corner, perhaps a perk of being a doctor.

Only as Anton kicked off his shoes and lay down on the bunk did he notice his painting of the coach house fixed pride of place above the entrance. Stephen's home. Or rather, their home, now that Anton was taking care of the place.

And until he turned his head on the pillow, neither had he noticed the photograph pinned to the side of the small rattan table next to the bed, of Anton and Stephen at the restaurant, with Anton laughing happily into the camera and Stephen's arm across his shoulders, grinning at him. The last thing the doctor would see at night before sleeping, the first as he woke.

After a deep, satisfying sigh, Anton closed his eyes, smelling faint traces of Stephen in the room, in the pillow and sheets.

"Don't worry, Sebastian," he murmured, drifting off to sleep. "He's in safe hands now."

BRIAN LANCASTER once believed that writing gay romantic fiction would be easy and cathartic. He also believed in Santa Claus and the Jolly Green Giant. At least he still has fantasies about those two. Born in the rural South of England in a town with its own clock tower and cricket pitch, he moved to Hong Kong in 1998. Life went from calm and curious to fast and furious. On the upside, the people he has since met provide inspiration for a whole new cast of characters in his stories. He also has his long-term, long-suffering partner and two cats to keep him grounded.

After winning two short story competitions in 2006 and being published in a compendium, he decided to dive into writing full-length novels. Diving proved to be easy, the challenge has been in treading water and trying to remain afloat.

Cynical enough to be classed a curable romantic, he is not seeking an antidote. When not working or writing, he enjoys acting in community theater productions, composing music, hosting pub quizzes, and any socializing that involves Chardonnay. And for the record, he would like to remind all those self-righteous white wine drinkers that White Burgundy, Chablis, and Champagne are still essentially Chardonnays

Also from Dreamspinner Press

BEYOND OBSESSION

JohnSIMPSON / RobertCUMMINGS

www.dreamspinnerpress.com

I'll Still Be There

KEELAN ELLIS

Also from Dreamspinner Press

Also from Dreamspinner Press

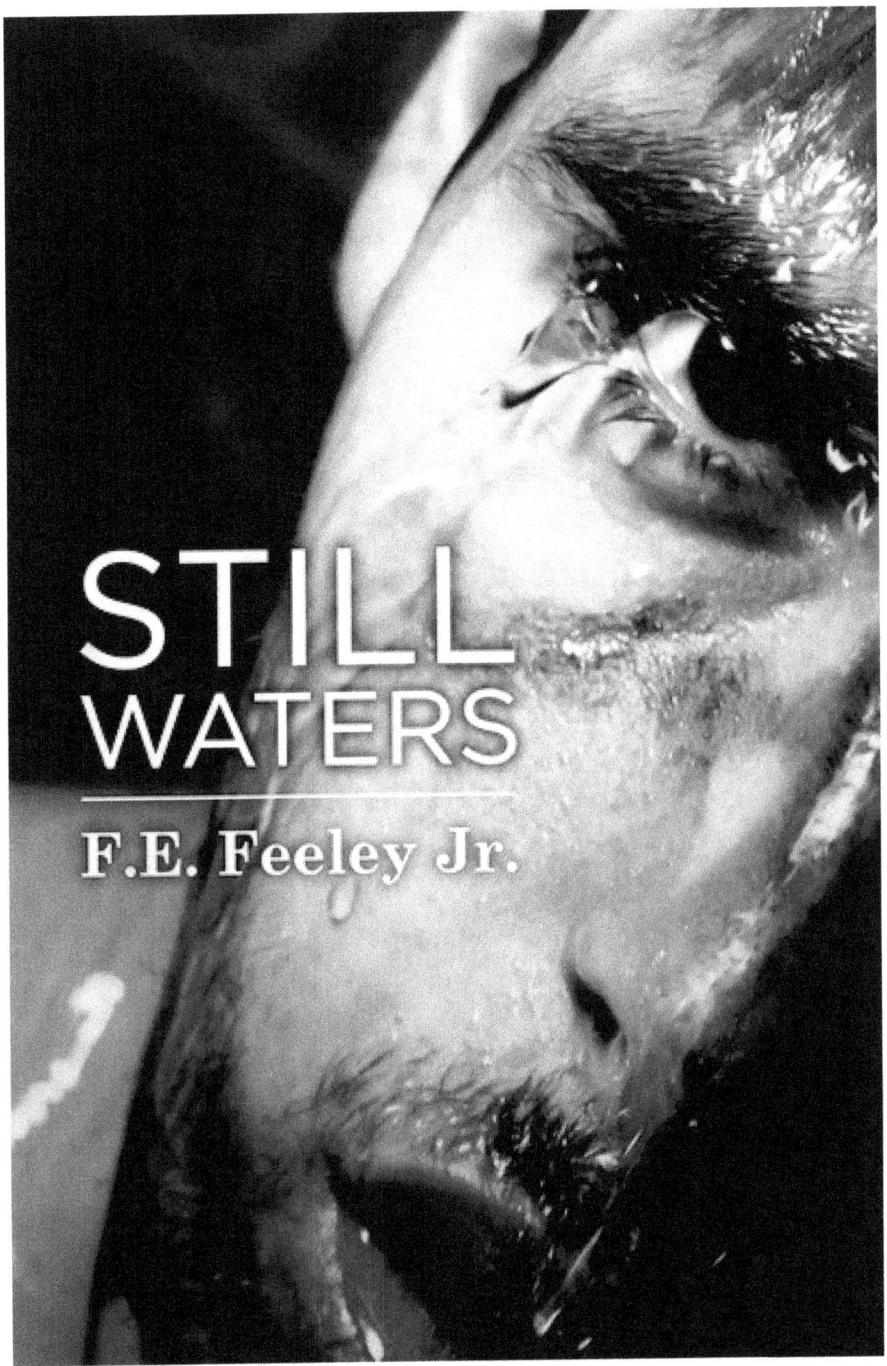

STILL
WATERS

F.E. Feeley Jr.

www.dreamspinnerpress.com